• CUBE KID •

DIARY OF AN 8-BIT WARRIOR
GRAPHIC NOVEL

WITHDRAWN

AN OP ALLIANCE

STORY ADAPTED BY
PIRATE SOURCIL

ILLUSTRATED BY
JEZ
◆
COLORED BY
ODONE

Andrews McMeel
PUBLISHING®

Thank you, Jez and Joël, for taking my ideas and
expressing them perfectly in art and color!
Thanks also to my family, Marion, and to
Anne-Charlotte for her steady support!
THOMAS

Thanks to my loved ones, Maite and Meryl, for their support.
Thanks also to the dream team, Thomas, Joël, and
Anne-Charlotte. It was great working with you!
And thank you, Cube Kid, for letting us play in your universe!
JEZ

Translated and based on the series of novels originally created
by Cube Kid © 404 éditions, a department of Édi8. Text by Pirate
Sourcil and illustrations by Jez © 2019 Editions Jungle/ Édi8.

Minecraft is a Notch Development AB registered trademark. This book
is a work of fiction and not an official Minecraft product, nor approved
by or associated with Mojang. The other names, characters, places,
and plots are either imagined by the author or used fictitiously.

Andrews McMeel Publishing
a division of Andrews McMeel Universal
1130 Walnut Street, Kansas City, Missouri 64106
www.andrewsmcmeel.com

21 22 23 24 25 SDB 10 9 8 7 6 5 4 3 2 1

ISBN: 978-1-5248-6316-6 (Paperback)
ISBN: 978-1-5248-6757-7 (Hardback)

Library of Congress Control Number: 2020945405

Made by:
King Yip (Dongguan) Printing & Packaging Factory Ltd.
Address and location of manufacturer:
Daning Administrative District, Humen Town
Dongguan Guangdong, China 523930
1st printing—11/23/20

ATTENTION: SCHOOLS AND BUSINESSES
Andrews McMeel books are available at quantity discounts with
bulk purchase for educational, business, or sales promotional use.
For information, please e-mail the Andrews McMeel Publishing
Special Sales Department: specialsales@amuniversal.com.

PART ONE

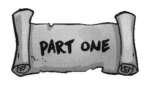

A NEW WARRIOR

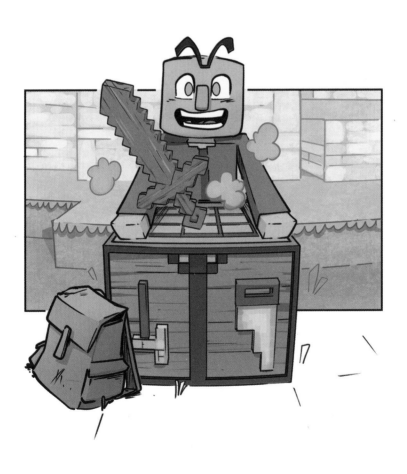

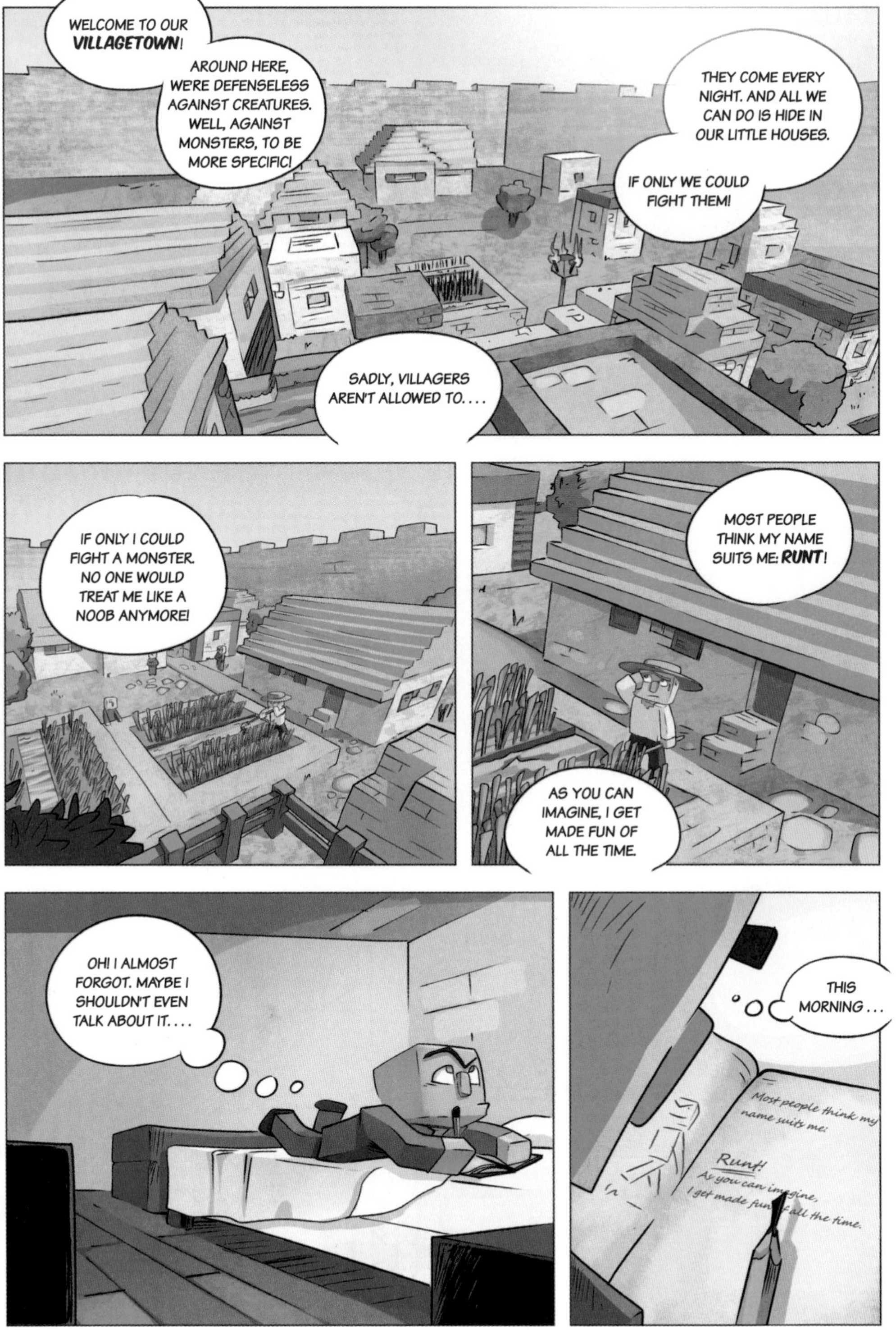
WELCOME TO OUR VILLAGETOWN!
AROUND HERE, WE'RE DEFENSELESS AGAINST CREATURES. WELL, AGAINST MONSTERS, TO BE MORE SPECIFIC!
THEY COME EVERY NIGHT. AND ALL WE CAN DO IS HIDE IN OUR LITTLE HOUSES.
IF ONLY WE COULD FIGHT THEM!
SADLY, VILLAGERS AREN'T ALLOWED TO. . . .
IF ONLY I COULD FIGHT A MONSTER. NO ONE WOULD TREAT ME LIKE A NOOB ANYMORE!
MOST PEOPLE THINK MY NAME SUITS ME: RUNT!
AS YOU CAN IMAGINE, I GET MADE FUN OF ALL THE TIME.
OH! I ALMOST FORGOT. MAYBE I SHOULDN'T EVEN TALK ABOUT IT. . . .
THIS MORNING . . .
Most people think my name suits me:
Runt!
As you can imagine, I get made fun of all the time.

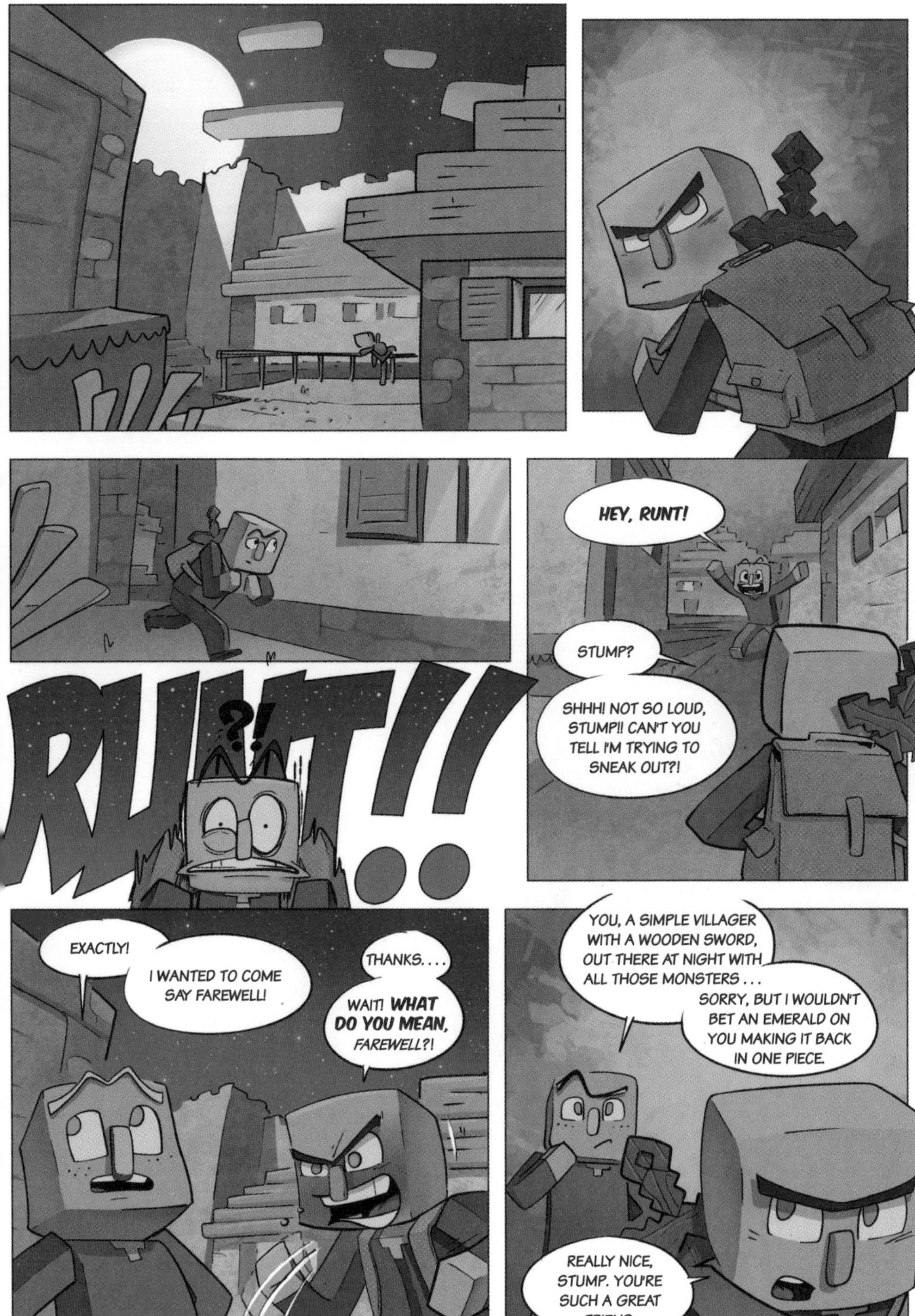
HEY, RUNT!
STUMP?
SHHH! NOT SO LOUD, STUMP!! CAN'T YOU TELL I'M TRYING TO SNEAK OUT?!
RUNT!!
?!
..
EXACTLY!
I WANTED TO COME SAY FAREWELL!
THANKS. . . .
WAIT! WHAT DO YOU MEAN, FAREWELL?!
YOU, A SIMPLE VILLAGER WITH A WOODEN SWORD, OUT THERE AT NIGHT WITH ALL THOSE MONSTERS . . .
SORRY, BUT I WOULDN'T BET AN EMERALD ON YOU MAKING IT BACK IN ONE PIECE.
REALLY NICE, STUMP. YOU'RE SUCH A GREAT FRIEND.

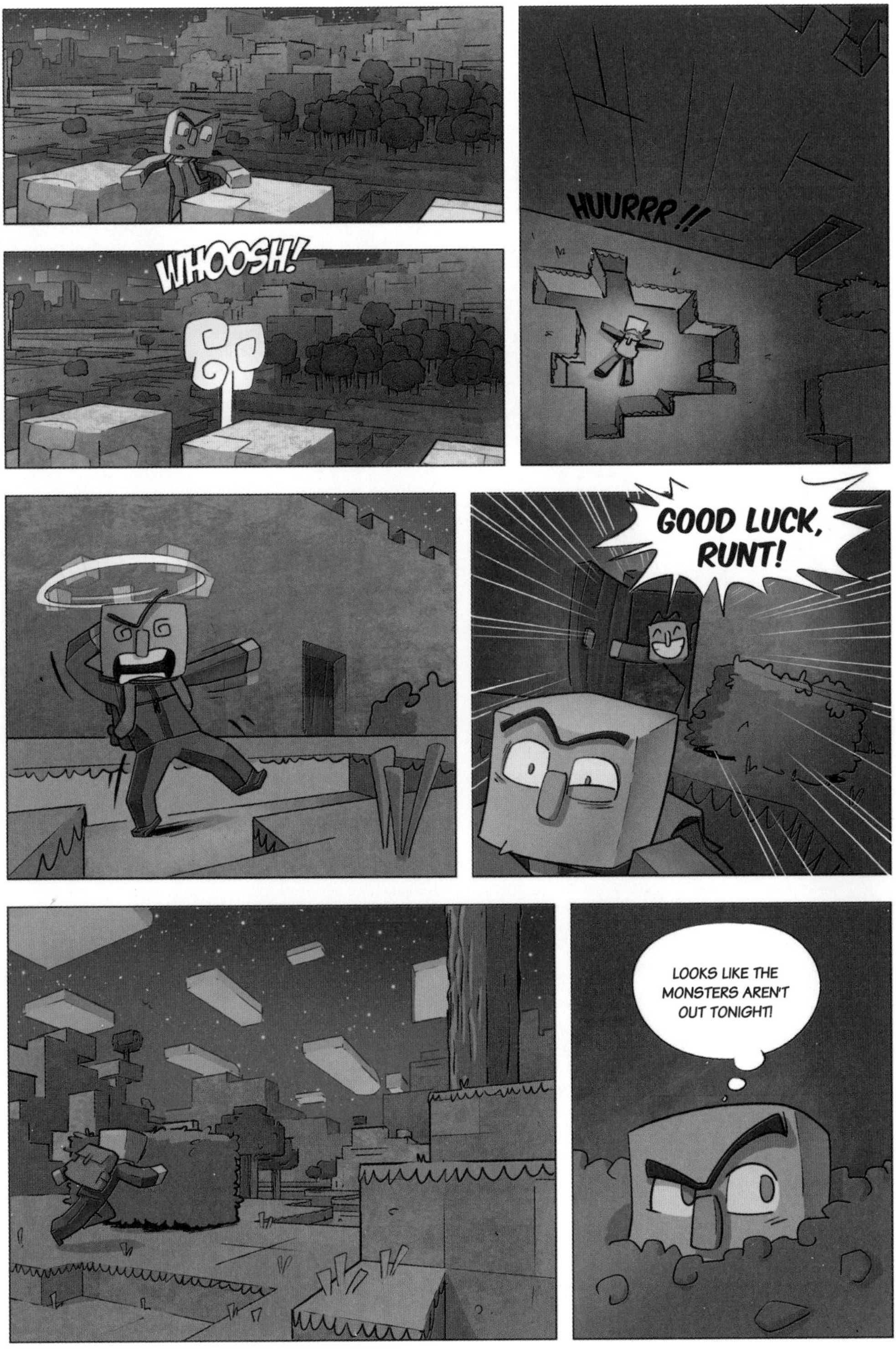
WHOOSH!
HUURRR!!
GOOD LUCK, RUNT!
LOOKS LIKE THE MONSTERS AREN'T OUT TONIGHT!

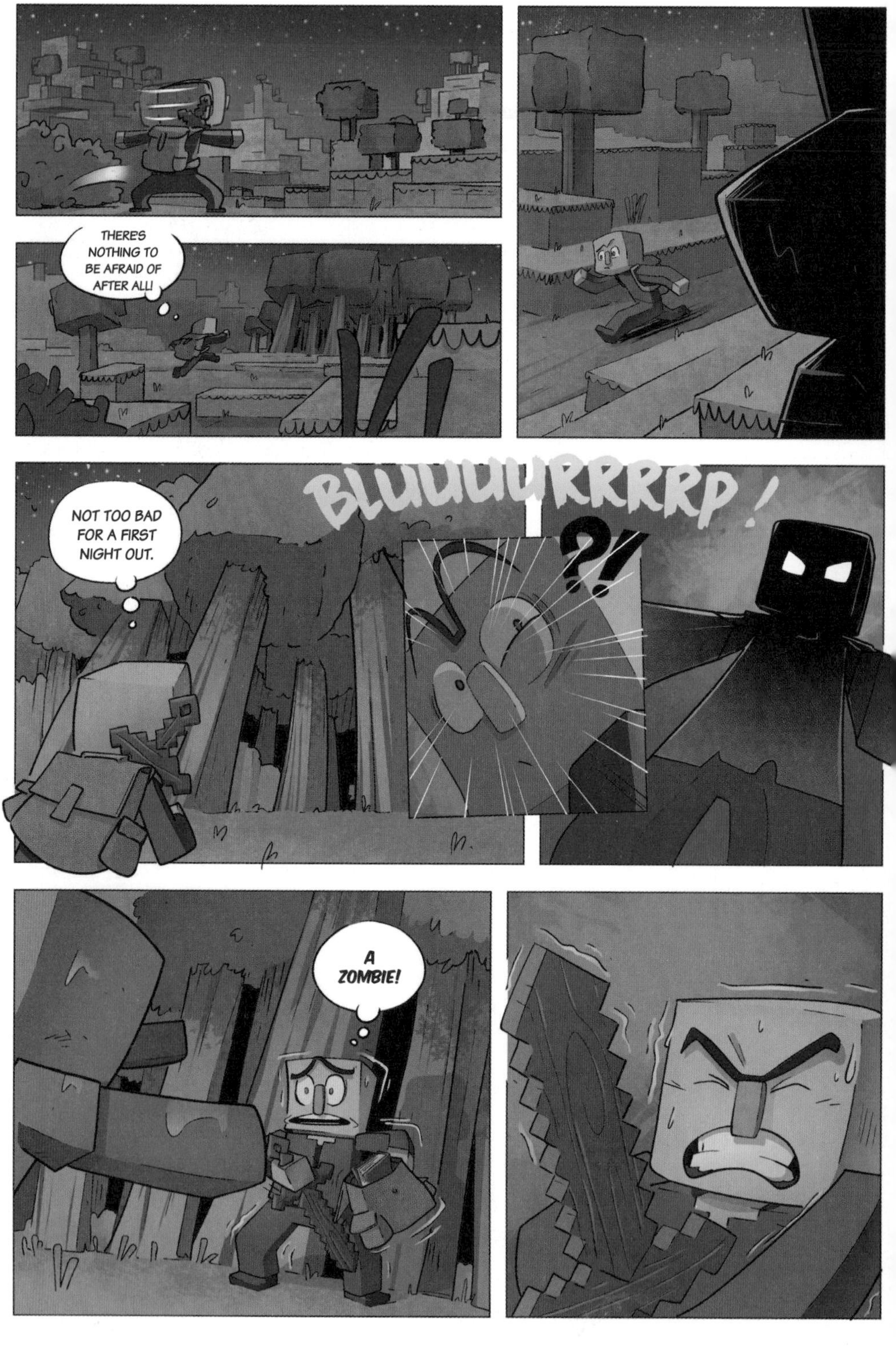

THERE'S NOTHING TO BE AFRAID OF AFTER ALL!
NOT TOO BAD FOR A FIRST NIGHT OUT.
BLUUUURRRRP!
?!
A ZOMBIE!

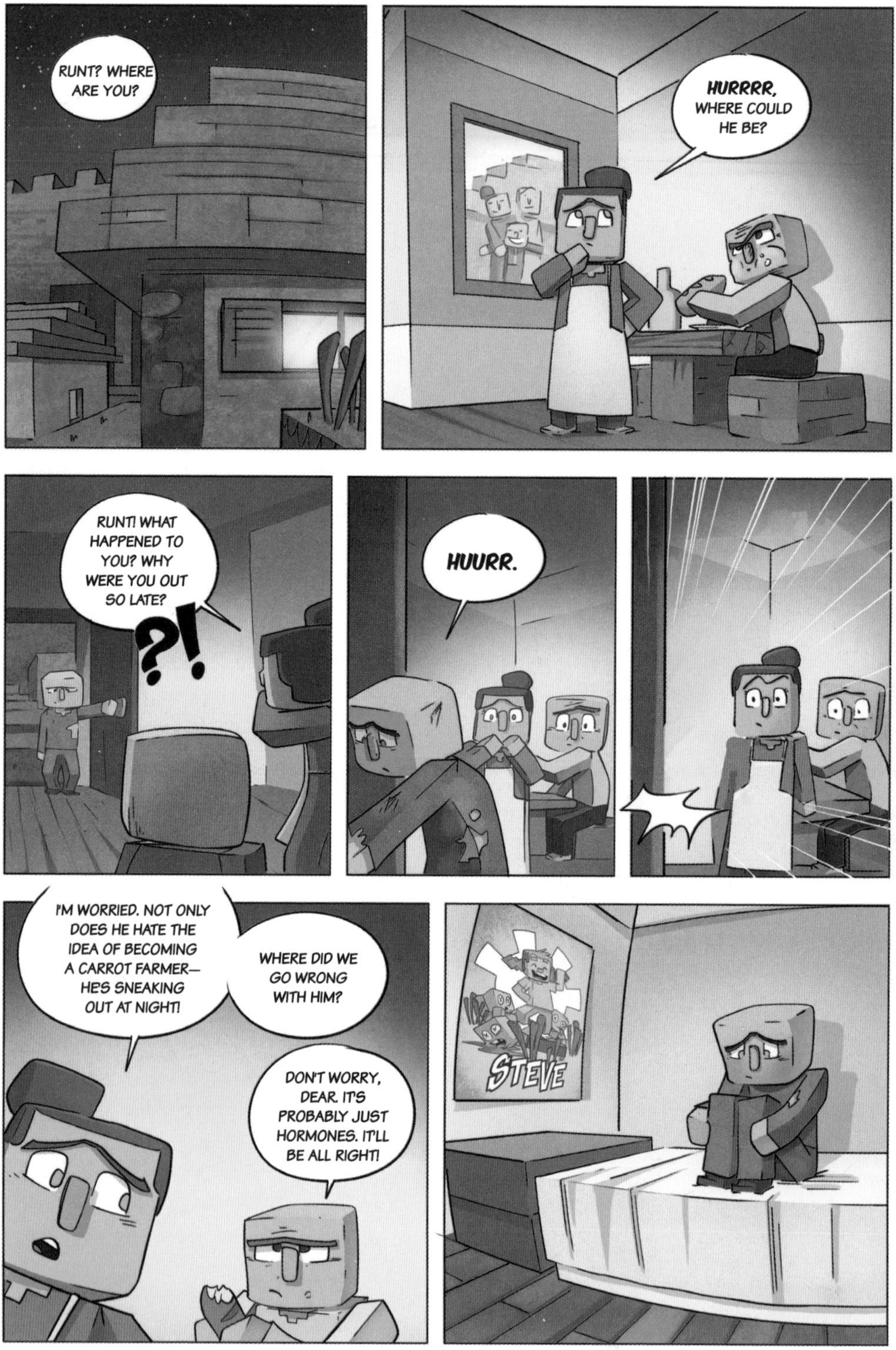
RUNT? WHERE ARE YOU?
HURRRR, WHERE COULD HE BE?
RUNT! WHAT HAPPENED TO YOU? WHY WERE YOU OUT SO LATE?
?!
HUURR.
I'M WORRIED. NOT ONLY DOES HE HATE THE IDEA OF BECOMING A CARROT FARMER—HE'S SNEAKING OUT AT NIGHT!
WHERE DID WE GO WRONG WITH HIM?
DON'T WORRY, DEAR. IT'S PROBABLY JUST HORMONES. IT'LL BE ALL RIGHT!
STEVE

HEY, HE MUST HAVE DROPPED HIS BAG WHEN HE RAN AWAY.

A DIARY? LOOKS LIKE I'M FINALLY GOING TO LEARN ALL ABOUT VILLAGERS!

BLURP?! WHAT HAPPENED TO YOU? WHY ARE YOU HOME SO EARLY?

?!

BLURRP!

SLAM!

I'M WORRIED!

NOT ONLY IS HE HATE-WANDERING AROUND AT NIGHT— HE DOESN'T EVEN WANT TO ATTACK VILLAGERS!

WHERE DID WE GO WRONG WITH HIM?

OH, IT'S PROBABLY JUST HIS ZOMBIE HORMONES.

DON'T WORRY, DEAR. IT'LL BE ALL RIGHT!

SEVERAL NIGHTS LATER . . .

LET'S SEE WHETHER YOU'VE BEEN PAYING ATTENTION.

LESSON 1: ATTACKING!

WHAT SHOULD YOU DO IF YOU RUN INTO A WARRIOR?

I KNOW! I KNOW!

YES, GLURP?

YOU RUN AT THEM, YELLING *EEEEEEEUUUUUUUH!*

VERY GOOD, GLURP!

A ZOMBIE-WARRIOR LOVE STORY?

I CAN'T READ THIS . . . BUT I KNOW IT'S LAME!

RIIIIP!

MAKING FRIENDS WITH OUR ENEMIES— HE DOESN'T DESERVE TO CALL HIMSELF A ZOMBIE! MORON!

HA! HA! HA! HA! HA! HA!

THEY'RE RIGHT. I DON'T BELONG HERE.

AT DAWN, ONCE EVERYONE IS ASLEEP, I'M OUT OF HERE FOR GOOD!

IT BURNS!

WITH THIS ON, I WON'T CATCH FIRE IN THE SUN.

A WARRIOR? WHERE?!

NO, NO, CREEPS, THERE'S NO WARRIOR!

Hiiiiiiisssssssss

HEY, CREEPS! IT'S ME, BLURP! SO YOU'RE ON WATCH DUTY, HUH?

SEE ANY WARRIORS?

?!

BOOM!

MAN, THEY'RE DUMB!

SO MUCH FOR SNEAKING OUT QUIETLY. . . .

I'VE GOT TO GET OUT OF HERE!

Monday

Tuesday

Wednesday

Thursday

IT MIGHT BE SMARTER TO GO BACK HOME AFTER ALL . . .

AWHILE LATER . . .

HELP! THIS CAVE IS FULL OF ZOMBIES!

OH NO! ANOTHER ONE?!

GO ON, TAKE A SEAT. MAKE YOURSELF COMFORTABLE!

NICE CAMP YOU'VE GOT HERE!

MY CRAFTING LESSONS FINALLY PAID OFF!

YOU LOOK LIKE YOU'RE STARVING! I'LL COOK A CHICKEN LEG FOR YOU!

THANKS, BUT YOU DON'T HAVE TO COOK IT FOR ME!

I LIKE RAW MEAT BETTER!

YOU'RE PRETTY WEIRD....

CUSTOMER'S ALWAYS RIGHT, I GUESS!

THANKS!

SO WHERE ARE YOU FROM ANYWAY? YOU'VE GOT A FUNNY ACCENT!

UMM...

FROM THE OTHER SIDE OF THE WORLD. I'VE WALKED A LONG WAY.

THAT'S SO COOL!

I JUST LEFT MY VILLAGE, ACTUALLY.

IMPRESSIVE! IS THAT WHY YOU WERE ON THE LOOKOUT FOR MONSTERS?

YEP!

I WANT TO BE THE FIRST VILLAGER TO BECOME A WARRIOR!

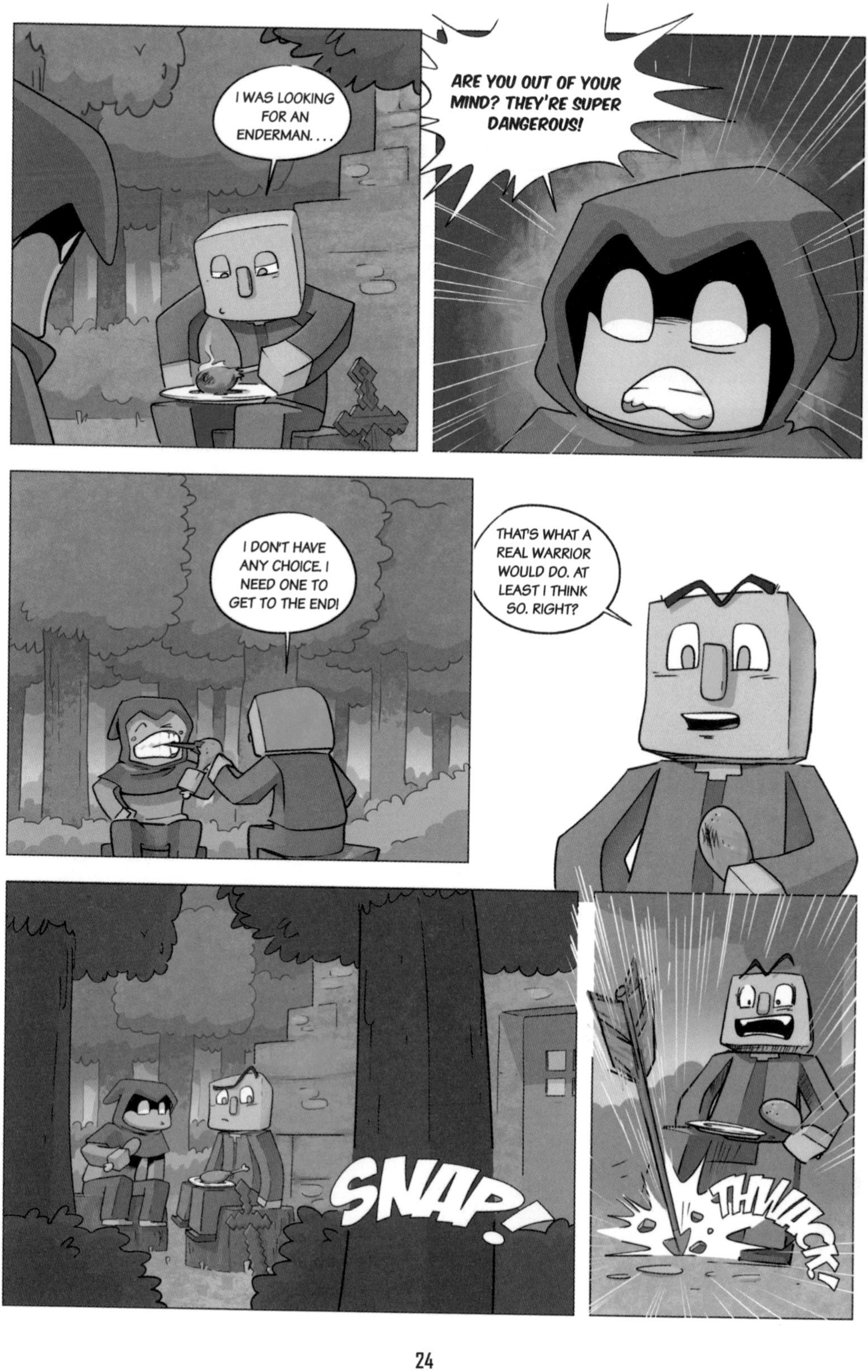
I WAS LOOKING FOR AN ENDERMAN. . . .
ARE YOU OUT OF YOUR MIND? THEY'RE SUPER DANGEROUS!
I DON'T HAVE ANY CHOICE. I NEED ONE TO GET TO THE END!
THAT'S WHAT A REAL WARRIOR WOULD DO. AT LEAST I THINK SO. RIGHT?
SNAP!
THWACK!

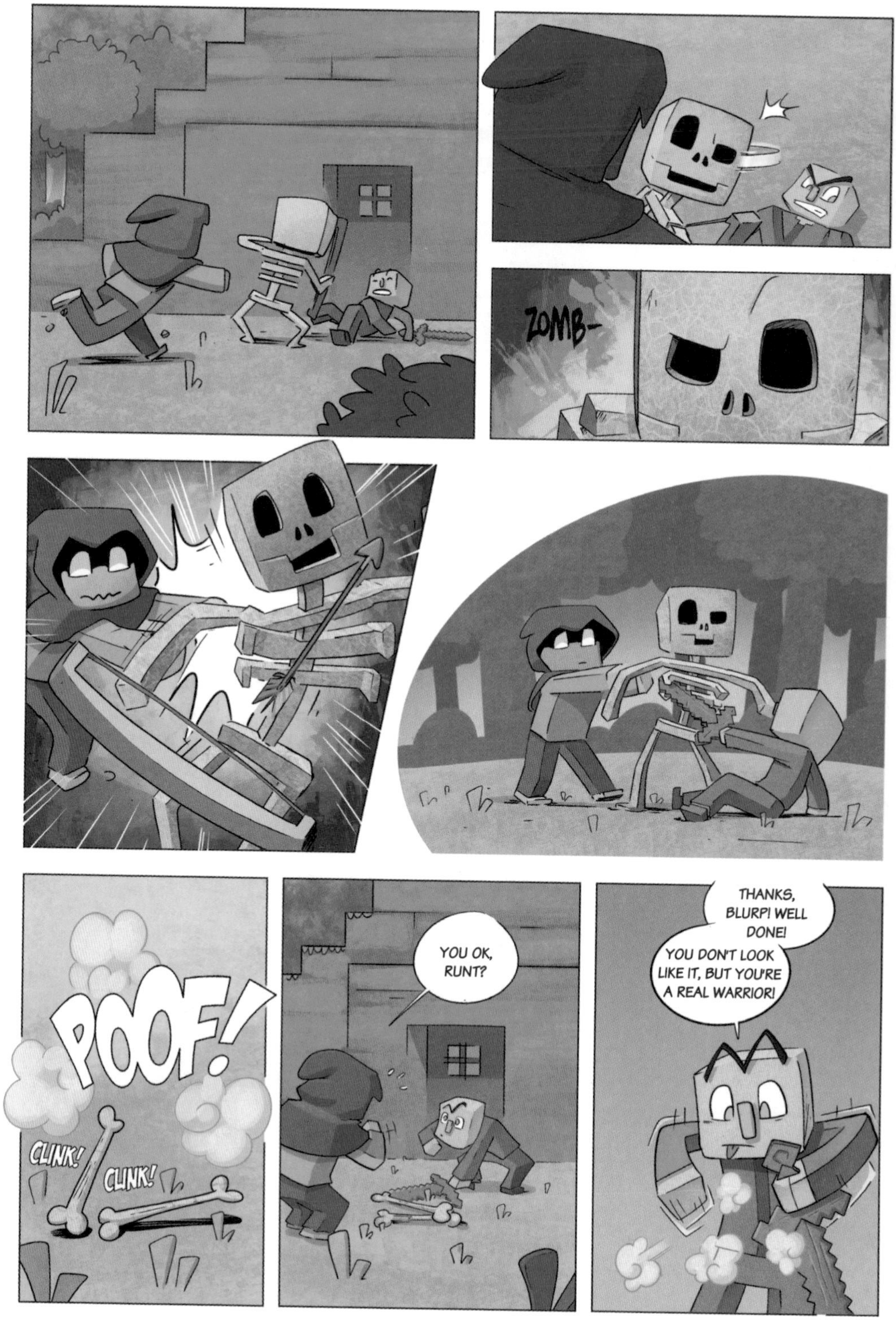
ZOMB-
POOF!
CLINK!
CLINK!
YOU OK, RUNT?
THANKS, BLURP! WELL DONE!
YOU DON'T LOOK LIKE IT, BUT YOU'RE A REAL WARRIOR!

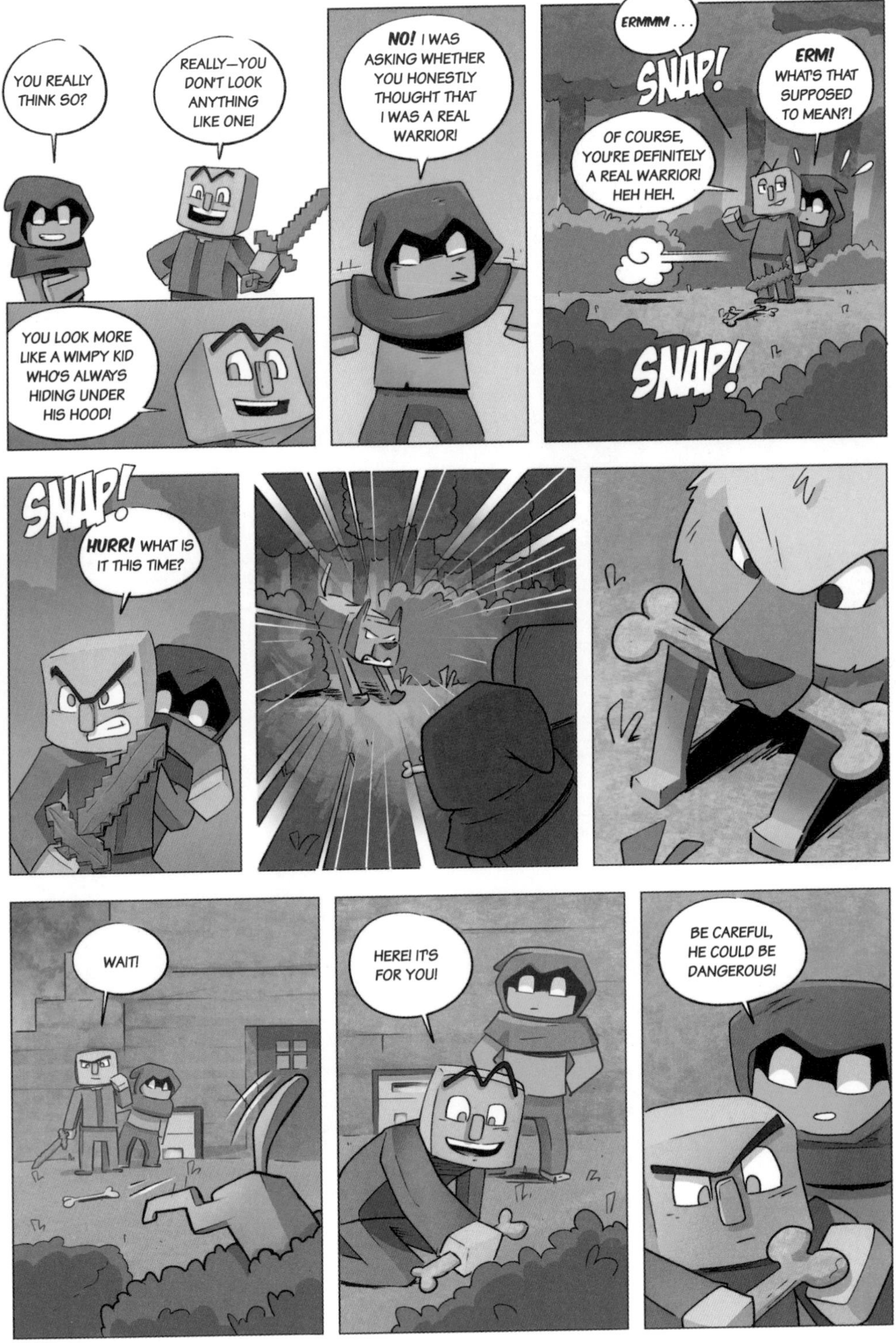
YOU REALLY THINK SO?
REALLY—YOU DON'T LOOK ANYTHING LIKE ONE!
YOU LOOK MORE LIKE A WIMPY KID WHO'S ALWAYS HIDING UNDER HIS HOOD!
NO! I WAS ASKING WHETHER YOU HONESTLY THOUGHT THAT I WAS A REAL WARRIOR!
ERMMM . . .
SNAP!
OF COURSE, YOU'RE DEFINITELY A REAL WARRIOR! HEH HEH.
ERM! WHAT'S THAT SUPPOSED TO MEAN?!
SNAP!
SNAP!
HURR! WHAT IS IT THIS TIME?
WAIT!
HERE! IT'S FOR YOU!
BE CAREFUL, HE COULD BE DANGEROUS!

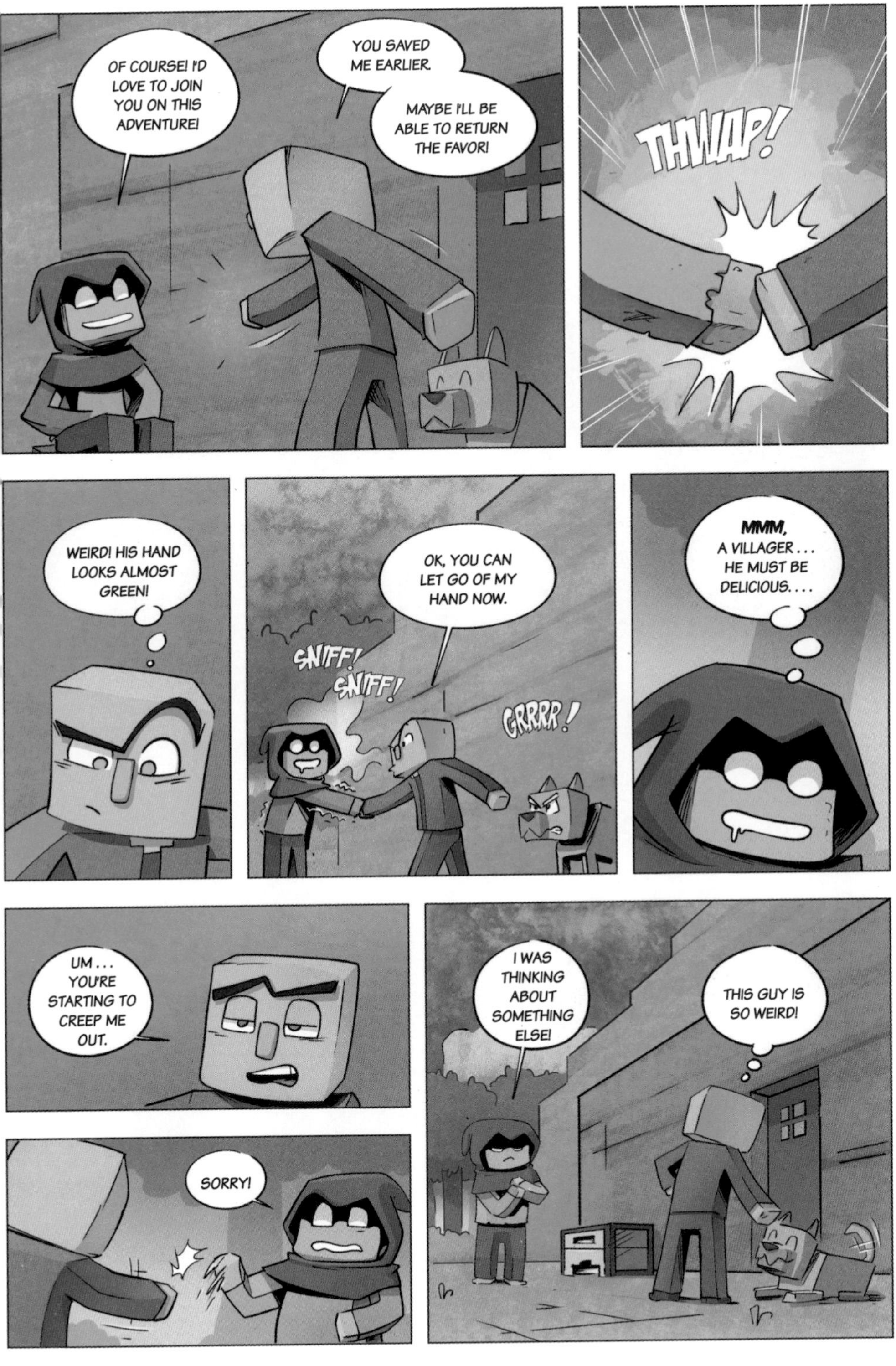
OF COURSE! I'D LOVE TO JOIN YOU ON THIS ADVENTURE!
YOU SAVED ME EARLIER.
MAYBE I'LL BE ABLE TO RETURN THE FAVOR!
THWAP!
WEIRD! HIS HAND LOOKS ALMOST GREEN!
OK, YOU CAN LET GO OF MY HAND NOW.
SNIFF!
SNIFF!
GRRRR!
MMM, A VILLAGER . . . HE MUST BE DELICIOUS. . . .
UM . . . YOU'RE STARTING TO CREEP ME OUT.
SORRY!
I WAS THINKING ABOUT SOMETHING ELSE!
THIS GUY IS SO WEIRD!

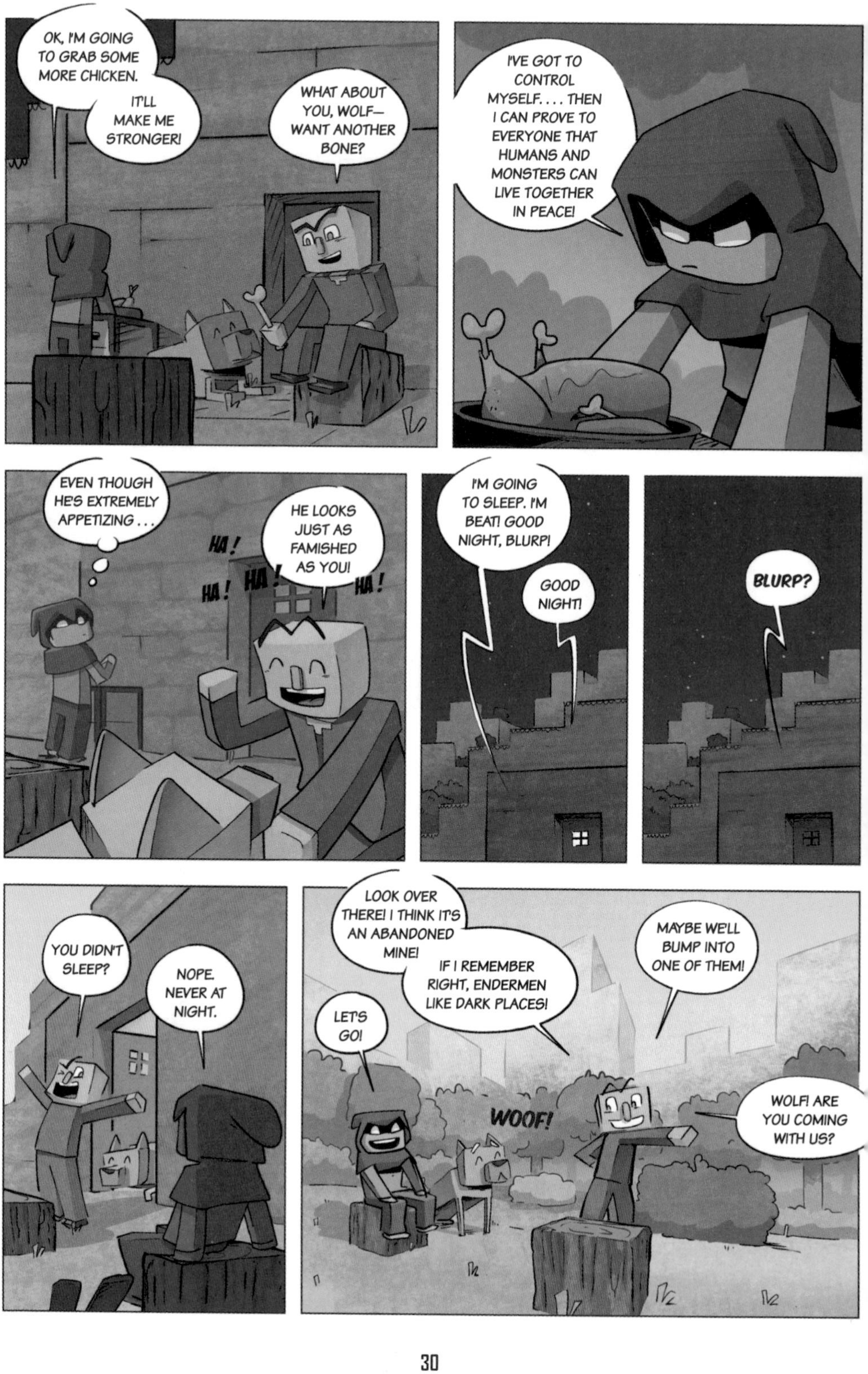
OK, I'M GOING TO GRAB SOME MORE CHICKEN.
IT'LL MAKE ME STRONGER!
WHAT ABOUT YOU, WOLF— WANT ANOTHER BONE?
I'VE GOT TO CONTROL MYSELF. . . . THEN I CAN PROVE TO EVERYONE THAT HUMANS AND MONSTERS CAN LIVE TOGETHER IN PEACE!
EVEN THOUGH HE'S EXTREMELY APPETIZING . . .
HA! HA! HA! HA!
HE LOOKS JUST AS FAMISHED AS YOU!
I'M GOING TO SLEEP. I'M BEAT! GOOD NIGHT, BLURP!
GOOD NIGHT!
BLURP?
YOU DIDN'T SLEEP?
NOPE. NEVER AT NIGHT.
LOOK OVER THERE! I THINK IT'S AN ABANDONED MINE!
IF I REMEMBER RIGHT, ENDERMEN LIKE DARK PLACES!
MAYBE WE'LL BUMP INTO ONE OF THEM!
LET'S GO!
WOOF!
WOLF! ARE YOU COMING WITH US?

DOES EVERYONE IN YOUR VILLAGE LOOK AS SICK AS YOU?

NOT AT ALL! WE AREN'T SICK! SOME OF US LOOK A BIT SCARY, BUT DEEP DOWN WE'RE GOOD PEOPLE!

YOU JUST HAVE TO DIG A LITTLE.

I WAS JUST KIDDING!

I HEAR YOU! IT'S THE SAME AT HOME FOR ME.

MY CRAFTING TEACHER IS TERRIFYING!

HERE, LOOK. IT'S A PICTURE OF MY FAMILY. I DIDN'T THINK I'D MISS THEM SO MUCH!

UM . . . IS THAT YOUR MOM?

NO, THAT'S MY DAD! DO YOU HAVE SLIME TURDS IN YOUR EYES OR SOMETHING?!

MY MOM'S NEXT TO HIM.

OH YEAH . . .

I THINK YOU NEED GLASSES, BLURP!

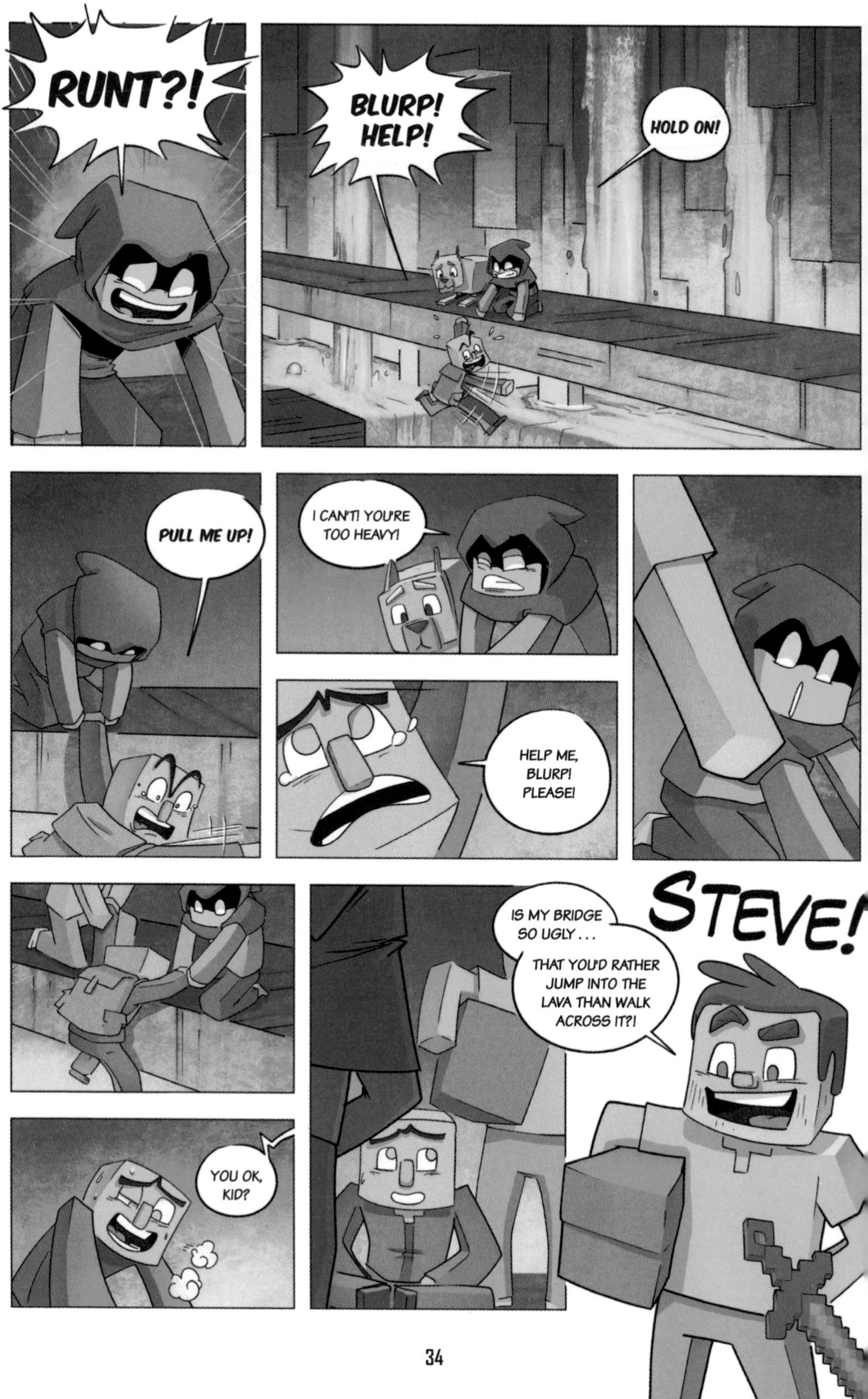
RUNT?!
BLURP! HELP!
HOLD ON!
PULL ME UP!
I CAN'T! YOU'RE TOO HEAVY!
HELP ME, BLURP! PLEASE!
YOU OK, KID?
IS MY BRIDGE SO UGLY . . .
THAT YOU'D RATHER JUMP INTO THE LAVA THAN WALK ACROSS IT?!
STEVE!

YOU TWO SHOULDN'T BE HANGING AROUND HERE. IT'S TOO DANGEROUS FOR KIDS.

WE'RE NOT KIDS, STEVE! WE'RE WARRIORS.

IF YOU SAY SO!

BUT YOU MIGHT WANT TO FOLLOW MY ADVICE. I WON'T ALWAYS BE THERE FOR YOU.

YOU ALL RIGHT, RUNT? ARE YOU SURE YOU WANT TO KEEP GOING?

STEVE MUST'VE ALREADY TAKEN OUT ALL THE MONSTERS AROUND HERE.

STILL, THIS IS TOO MUCH ADVENTURE FOR ONE DAY. LET'S GET OUT OF HERE!

AND LET'S DO IT WITHOUT BREAKING OUR NECKS. . . .

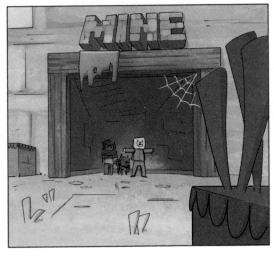

SAY, RUNT, WHY DID YOU RUN AWAY FROM HOME?

WELL... I ALWAYS WANTED TO BE A WARRIOR...

AND MY PARENTS WEREN'T OK WITH THAT...

I KNOW WHAT IT'S LIKE WHEN YOUR FAMILY DOESN'T ACCEPT WHO YOU ARE.

UM, YEAH. SOMETHING LIKE THAT.

ANYWAY, I'M GLAD I MET YOU.

IT'S HARD BEING ALONE OUT HERE.

DO YOURS WANT YOU TO STAY A REGULAR VILLAGER TOO?

YEAH, IT'S MORE FUN AS A TEAM!

YOU'RE A TRUE FRIEND, BLURP.

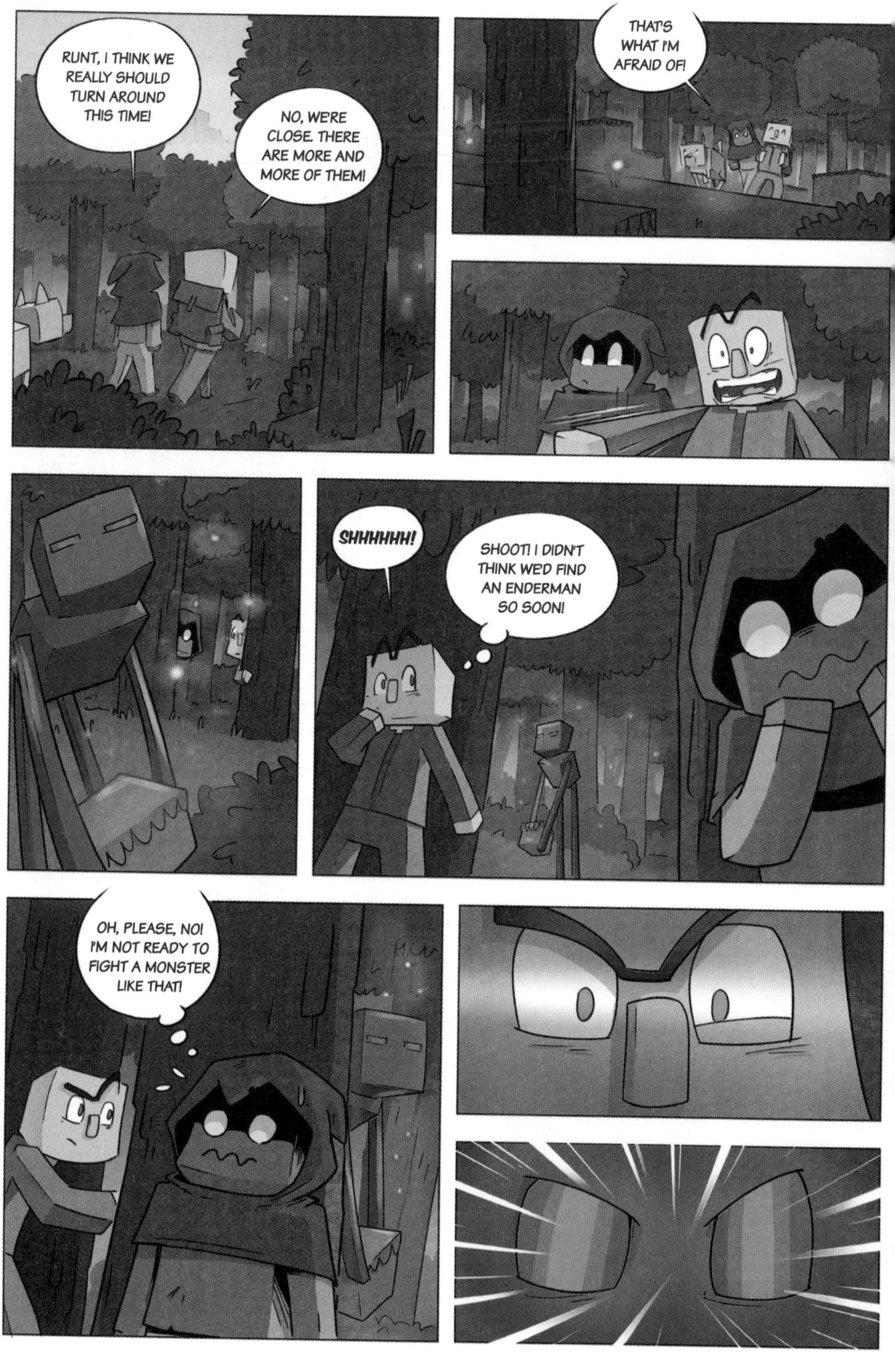
RUNT, I THINK WE REALLY SHOULD TURN AROUND THIS TIME!
NO, WE'RE CLOSE. THERE ARE MORE AND MORE OF THEM!
THAT'S WHAT I'M AFRAID OF!
SHHHHHH!
SHOOT! I DIDN'T THINK WE'D FIND AN ENDERMAN SO SOON!
OH, PLEASE, NO! I'M NOT READY TO FIGHT A MONSTER LIKE THAT!

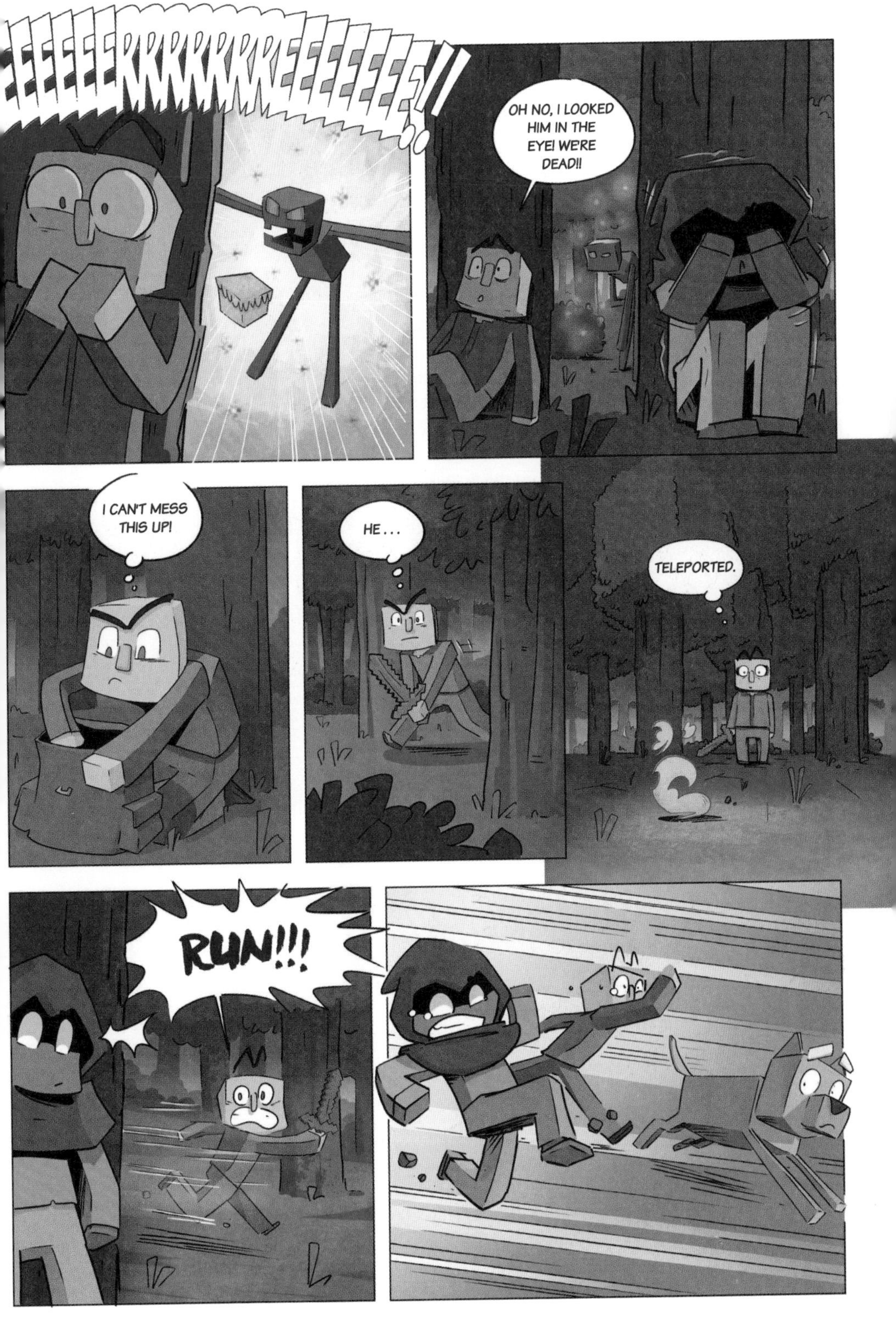
EEEEEERRRRRRRREEEEEEEE!!
OH NO, I LOOKED HIM IN THE EYE! WE'RE DEAD!!
I CAN'T MESS THIS UP!
HE . . .
TELEPORTED.
RUN!!!

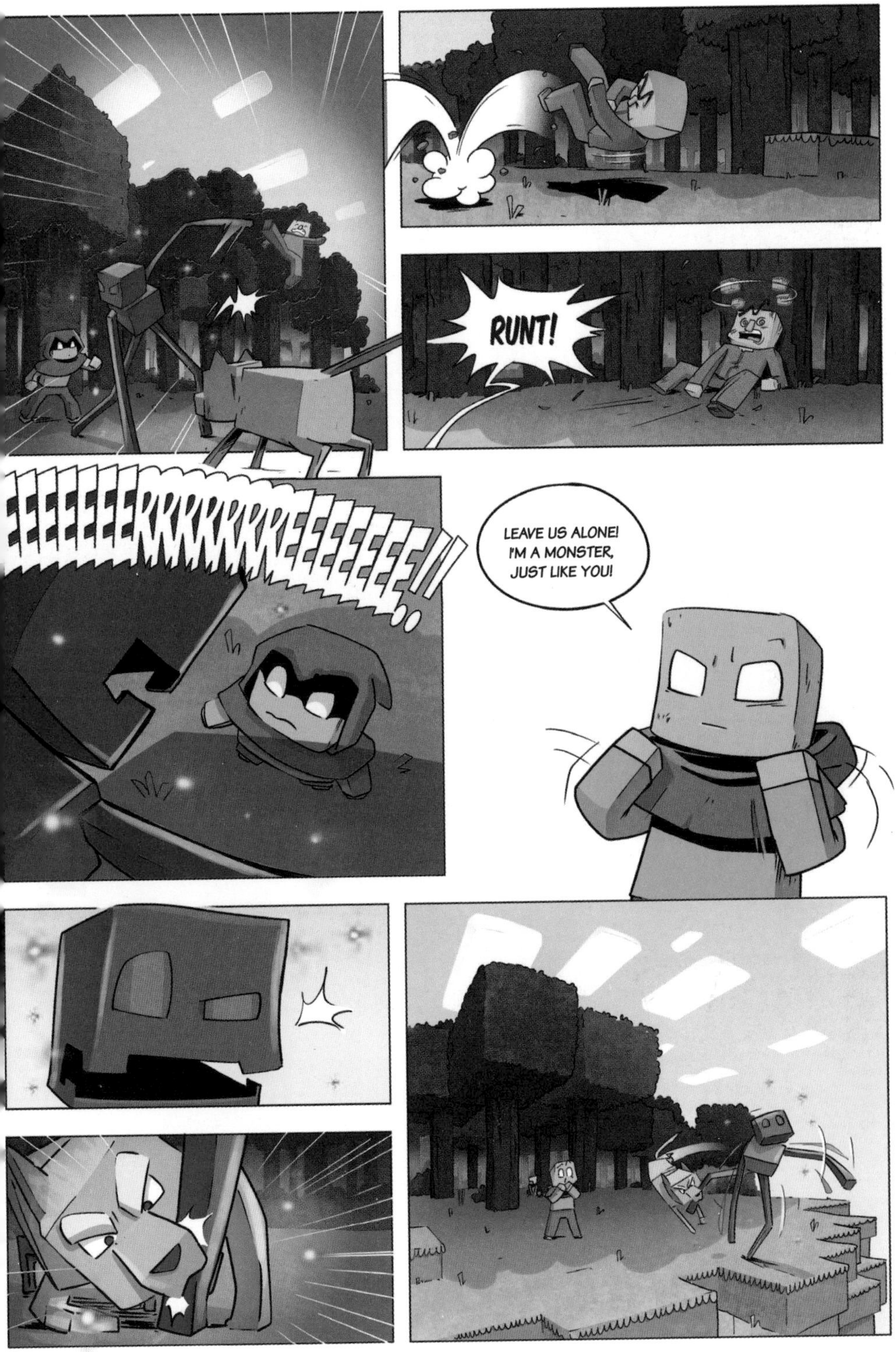
RUNT!
EEEEEEEERRRRRRRREEEEEEEE!!
LEAVE US ALONE! I'M A MONSTER, JUST LIKE YOU!

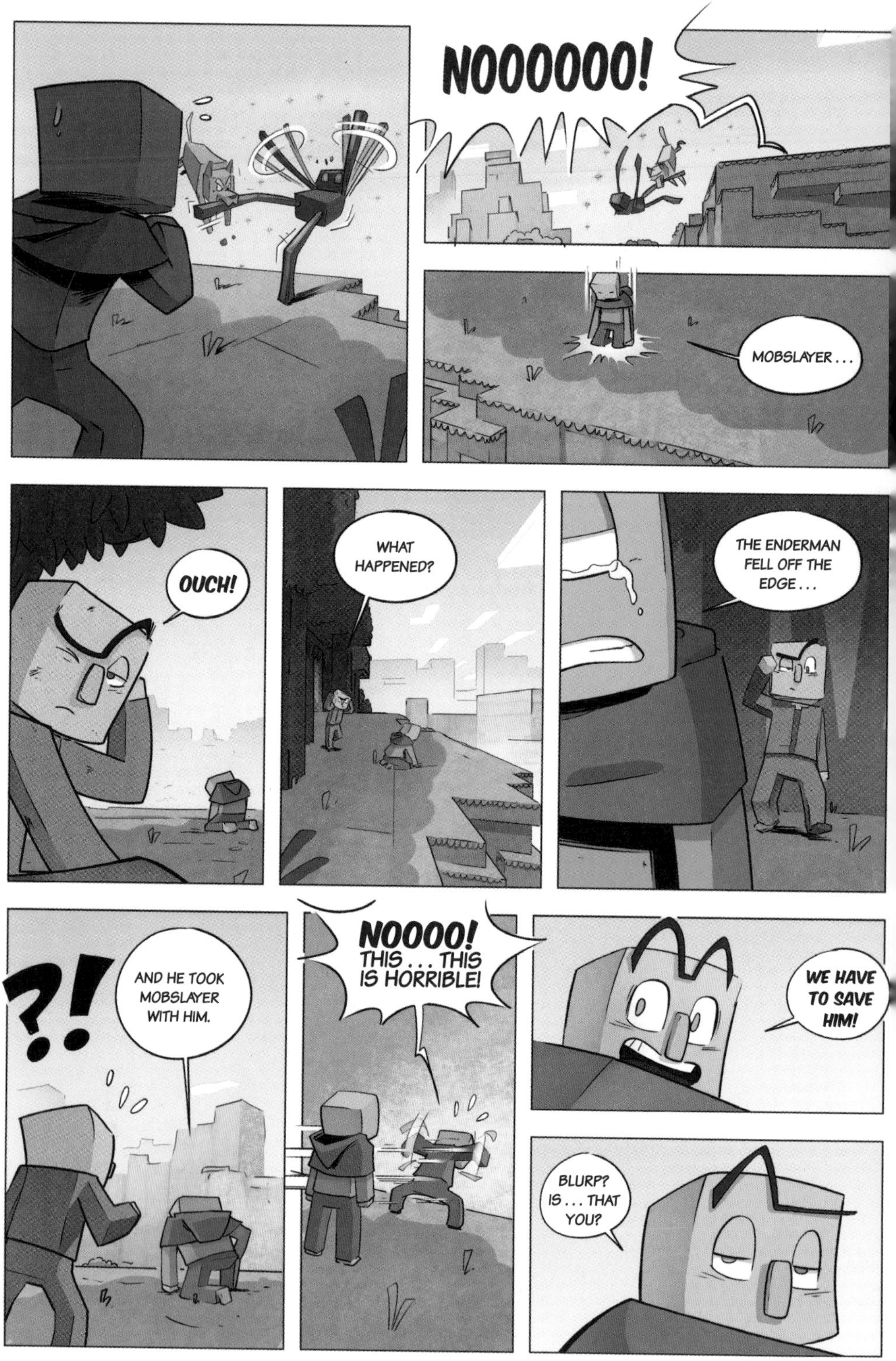
NOOOOOO!
MOBSLAYER . . .
OUCH!
WHAT HAPPENED?
THE ENDERMAN FELL OFF THE EDGE . . .
?!
AND HE TOOK MOBSLAYER WITH HIM.
NOOOO! THIS . . . THIS IS HORRIBLE!
WE HAVE TO SAVE HIM!
BLURP? IS . . . THAT YOU?

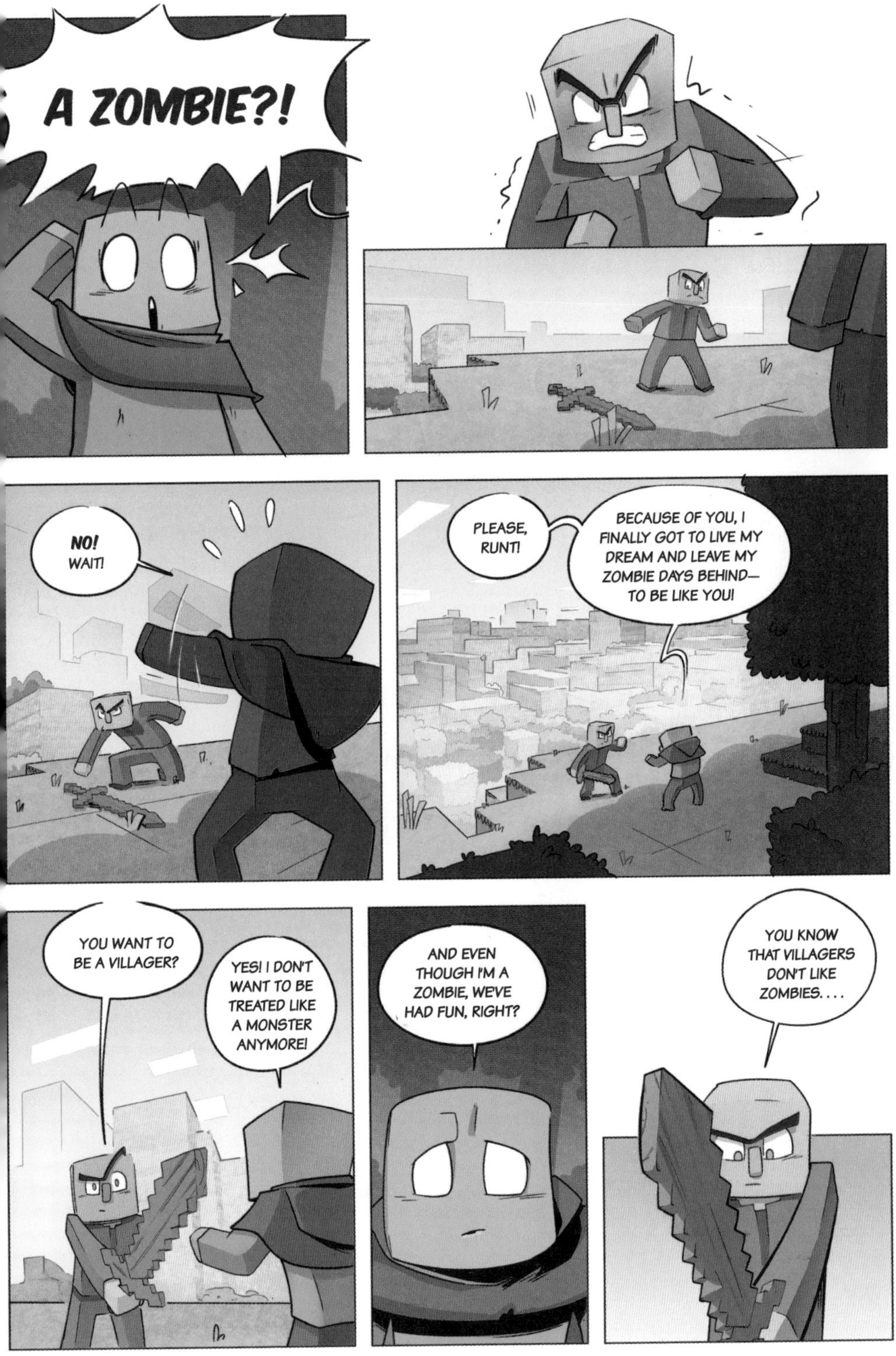
A ZOMBIE?!
NO! WAIT!
PLEASE, RUNT!
BECAUSE OF YOU, I FINALLY GOT TO LIVE MY DREAM AND LEAVE MY ZOMBIE DAYS BEHIND—TO BE LIKE YOU!
YOU WANT TO BE A VILLAGER?
YES! I DON'T WANT TO BE TREATED LIKE A MONSTER ANYMORE!
AND EVEN THOUGH I'M A ZOMBIE, WE'VE HAD FUN, RIGHT?
YOU KNOW THAT VILLAGERS DON'T LIKE ZOMBIES. . . .

PART TWO

A STROLL THROUGH THE NETHER

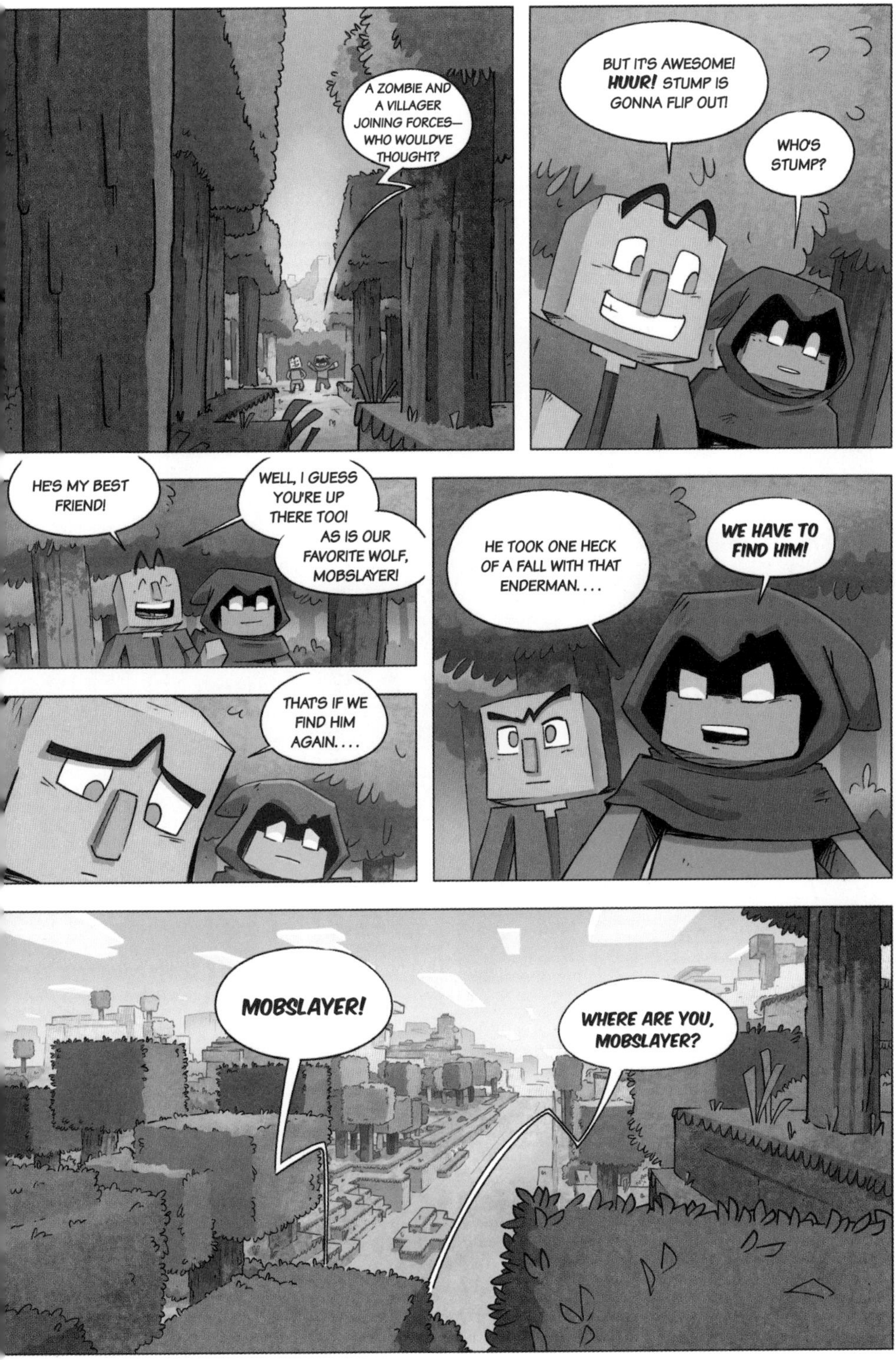
A ZOMBIE AND A VILLAGER JOINING FORCES—WHO WOULD'VE THOUGHT?
BUT IT'S AWESOME! **HUUR!** STUMP IS GONNA FLIP OUT!
WHO'S STUMP?
HE'S MY BEST FRIEND!
WELL, I GUESS YOU'RE UP THERE TOO!
AS IS OUR FAVORITE WOLF, MOBSLAYER!
THAT'S IF WE FIND HIM AGAIN. . . .
HE TOOK ONE HECK OF A FALL WITH THAT ENDERMAN. . . .
WE HAVE TO FIND HIM!
MOBSLAYER!
WHERE ARE YOU, MOBSLAYER?

AWESOME! OUR DEAR MOBSLAYER!

ACTUALLY... I DON'T THINK THIS IS HIM.

?! GRRR! GRRR!

THERE'S MORE!

BLURP, DO YOU STILL HAVE CHICKEN BONES IN YOUR INVENTORY?

GRRR

GRRR

NO... BUT I THINK IT'S OUR BONES THEY'RE AFTER!

I'VE GOT AN IDEA!

GRRR

RUN?

NO, A BETTER IDEA! I'M GOING TO PRETEND TO THROW A BONE REALLY FAR!

YOU'LL SEE. THEY'LL GO AFTER IT!

YUMMMMM! WHO WANTS A DELICIOUS BONE?

WHOOSH

FETCH!

GRRR

GRRR

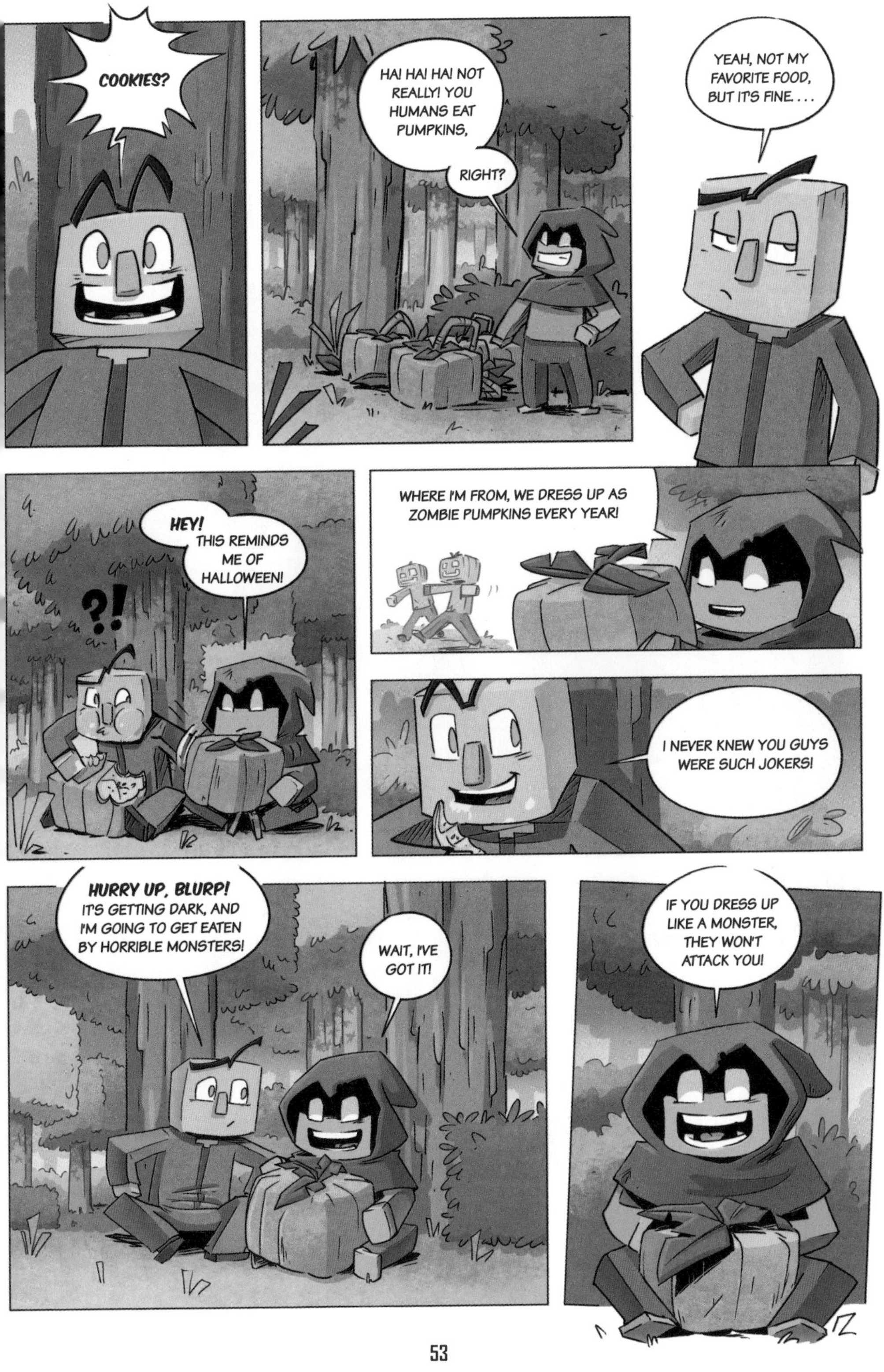
COOKIES?
HA! HA! HA! NOT REALLY! YOU HUMANS EAT PUMPKINS,
RIGHT?
YEAH, NOT MY FAVORITE FOOD, BUT IT'S FINE. . . .
HEY! THIS REMINDS ME OF HALLOWEEN!
?!
WHERE I'M FROM, WE DRESS UP AS ZOMBIE PUMPKINS EVERY YEAR!
I NEVER KNEW YOU GUYS WERE SUCH JOKERS!
HURRY UP, BLURP! IT'S GETTING DARK, AND I'M GOING TO GET EATEN BY HORRIBLE MONSTERS!
WAIT, I'VE GOT IT!
IF YOU DRESS UP LIKE A MONSTER, THEY WON'T ATTACK YOU!

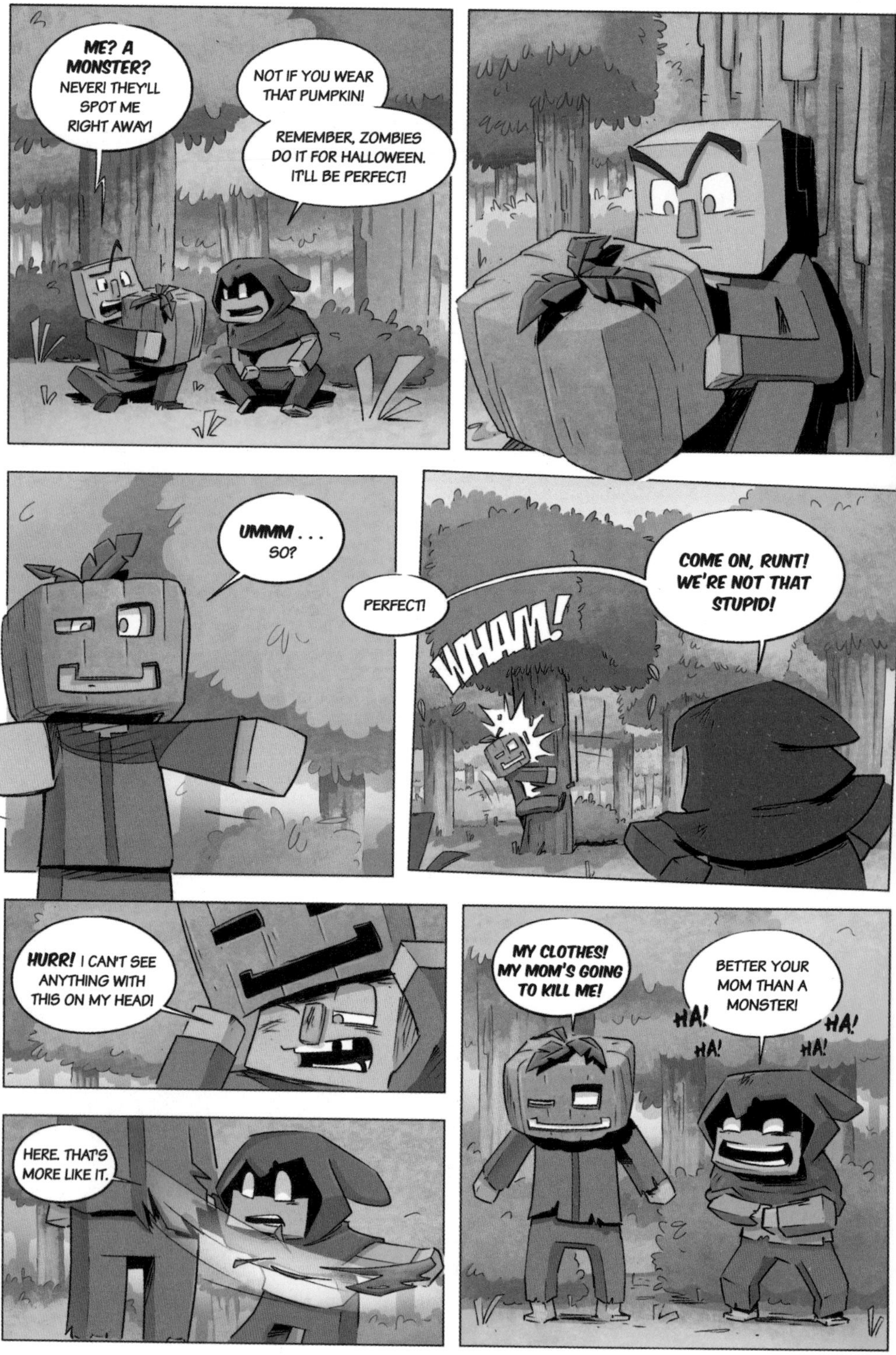
ME? A MONSTER? NEVER! THEY'LL SPOT ME RIGHT AWAY!
NOT IF YOU WEAR THAT PUMPKIN!
REMEMBER, ZOMBIES DO IT FOR HALLOWEEN. IT'LL BE PERFECT!
UMMM . . . SO?
PERFECT!
COME ON, RUNT! WE'RE NOT THAT STUPID!
WHAM!
HURR! I CAN'T SEE ANYTHING WITH THIS ON MY HEAD!
HERE. THAT'S MORE LIKE IT.
MY CLOTHES! MY MOM'S GOING TO KILL ME!
BETTER YOUR MOM THAN A MONSTER!
HA! HA! HA! HA!

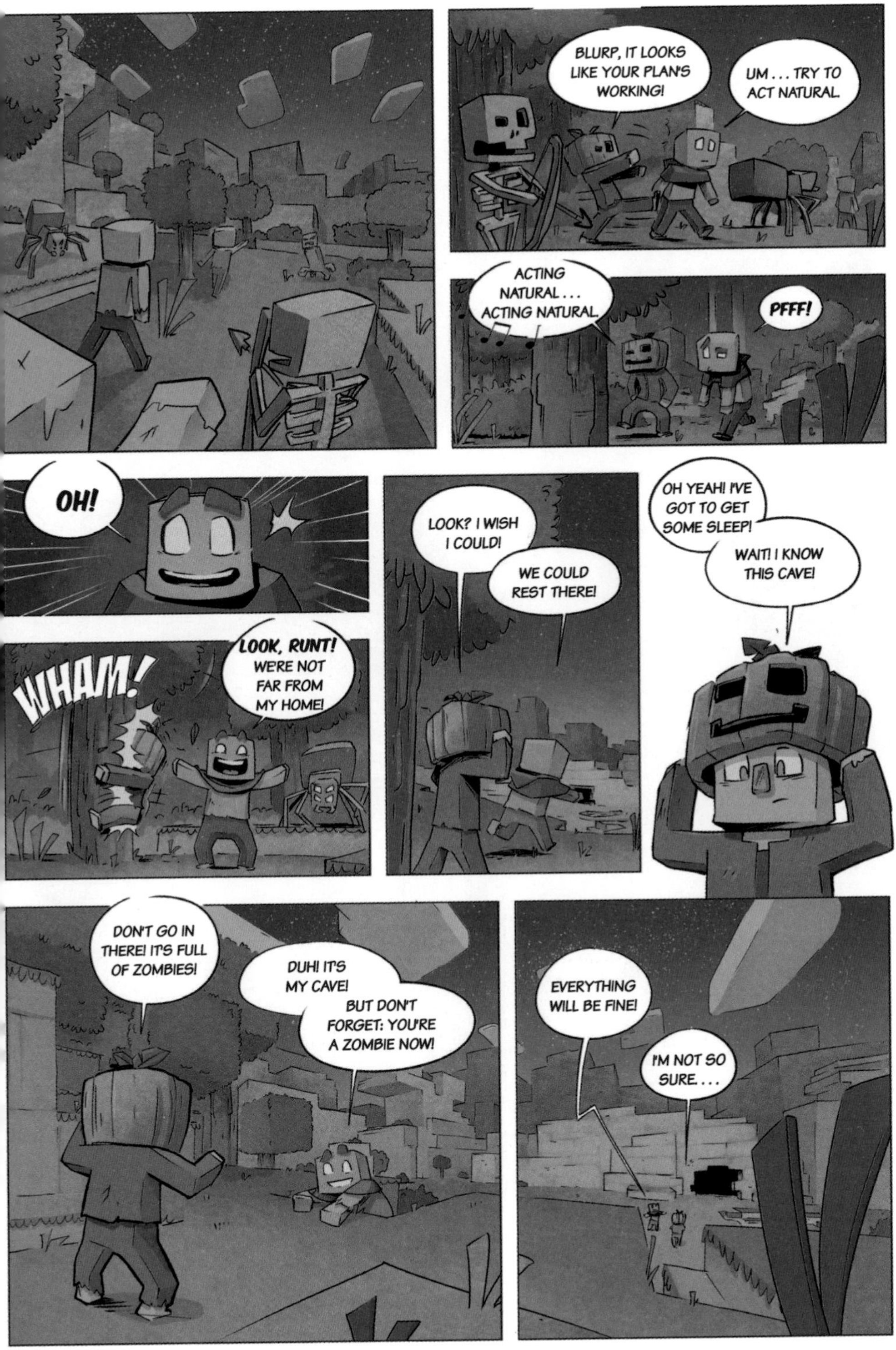
BLURP, IT LOOKS LIKE YOUR PLAN'S WORKING!
UM . . . TRY TO ACT NATURAL.
ACTING NATURAL . . . ACTING NATURAL.
PFFF!
OH!
WHAM!
LOOK, RUNT! WE'RE NOT FAR FROM MY HOME!
LOOK? I WISH I COULD!
WE COULD REST THERE!
OH YEAH! I'VE GOT TO GET SOME SLEEP!
WAIT! I KNOW THIS CAVE!
DON'T GO IN THERE! IT'S FULL OF ZOMBIES!
DUH! IT'S MY CAVE!
BUT DON'T FORGET: YOU'RE A ZOMBIE NOW!
EVERYTHING WILL BE FINE!
I'M NOT SO SURE. . . .

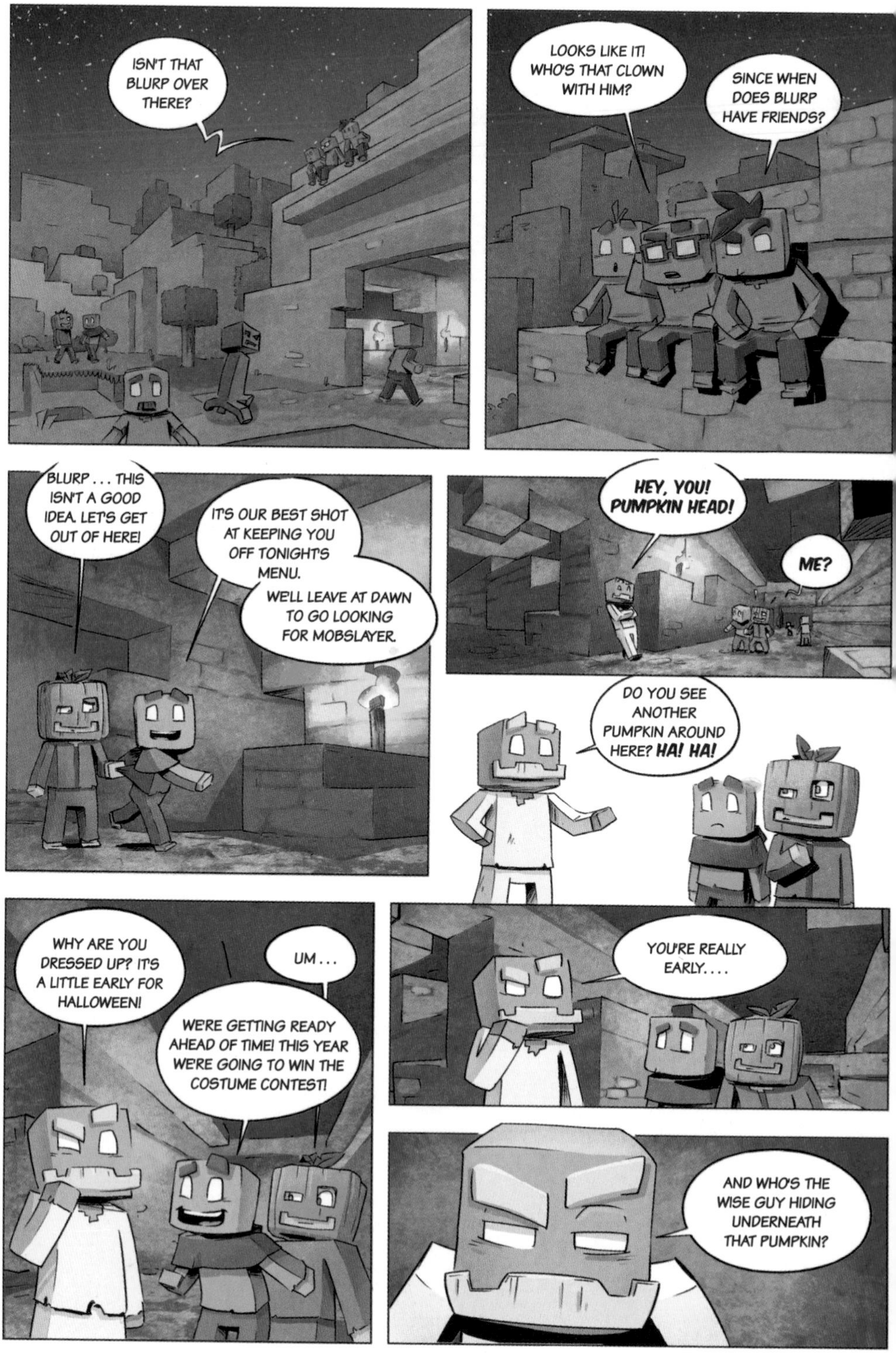
ISN'T THAT BLURP OVER THERE?
LOOKS LIKE IT! WHO'S THAT CLOWN WITH HIM?
SINCE WHEN DOES BLURP HAVE FRIENDS?
BLURP . . . THIS ISN'T A GOOD IDEA. LET'S GET OUT OF HERE!
IT'S OUR BEST SHOT AT KEEPING YOU OFF TONIGHT'S MENU.
WE'LL LEAVE AT DAWN TO GO LOOKING FOR MOBSLAYER.
HEY, YOU! PUMPKIN HEAD!
ME?
DO YOU SEE ANOTHER PUMPKIN AROUND HERE? HA! HA!
WHY ARE YOU DRESSED UP? IT'S A LITTLE EARLY FOR HALLOWEEN!
UM . . .
WE'RE GETTING READY AHEAD OF TIME! THIS YEAR WE'RE GOING TO WIN THE COSTUME CONTEST!
YOU'RE REALLY EARLY. . . .
AND WHO'S THE WISE GUY HIDING UNDERNEATH THAT PUMPKIN?

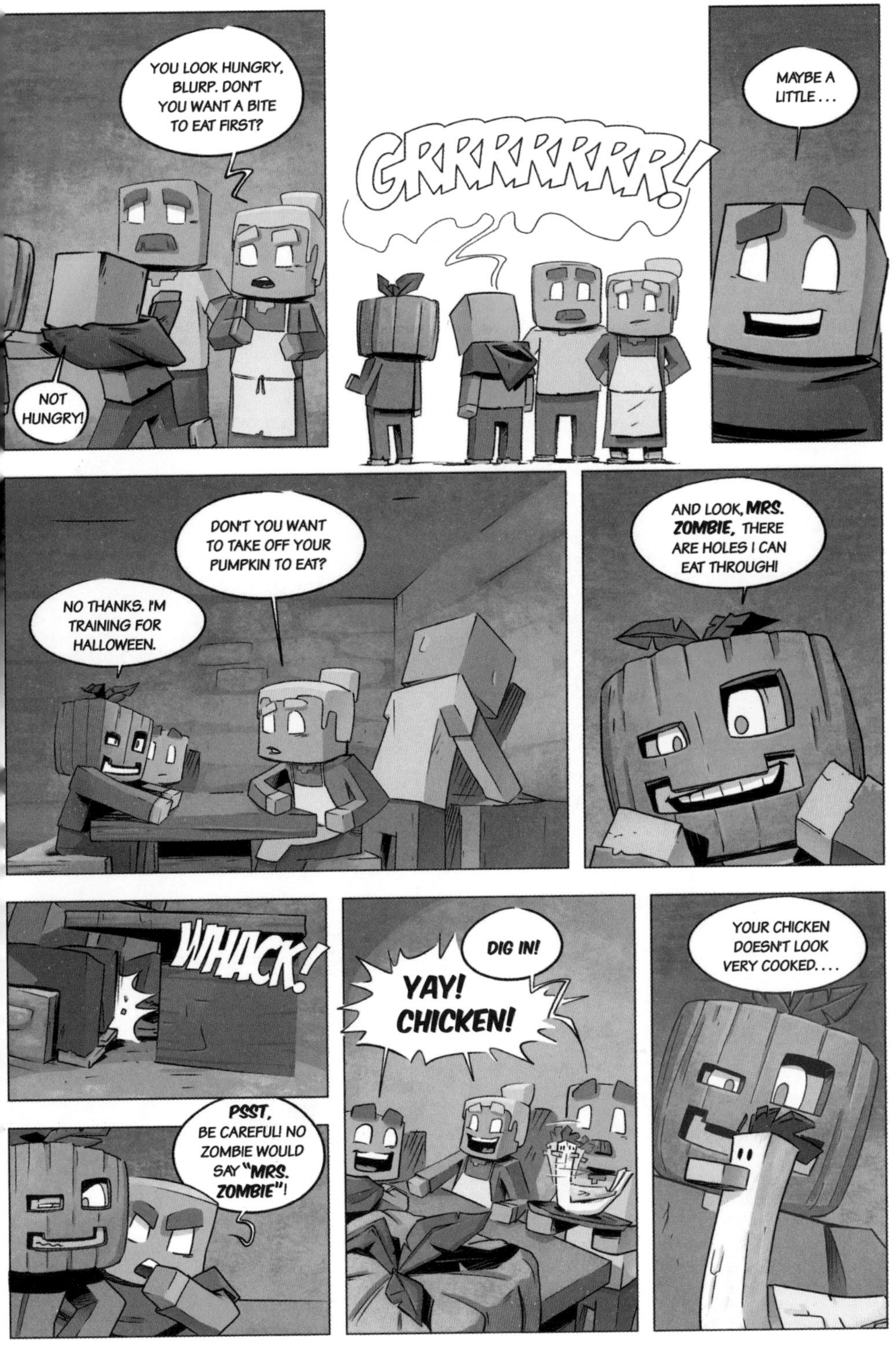
YOU LOOK HUNGRY, BLURP. DON'T YOU WANT A BITE TO EAT FIRST?
NOT HUNGRY!
GRRRRRRRR!
MAYBE A LITTLE . . .
DON'T YOU WANT TO TAKE OFF YOUR PUMPKIN TO EAT?
NO THANKS. I'M TRAINING FOR HALLOWEEN.
AND LOOK, **MRS. ZOMBIE,** THERE ARE HOLES I CAN EAT THROUGH!
WHACK!
PSST, BE CAREFUL! NO ZOMBIE WOULD SAY "**MRS. ZOMBIE**"!
DIG IN!
YAY! CHICKEN!
YOUR CHICKEN DOESN'T LOOK VERY COOKED. . . .

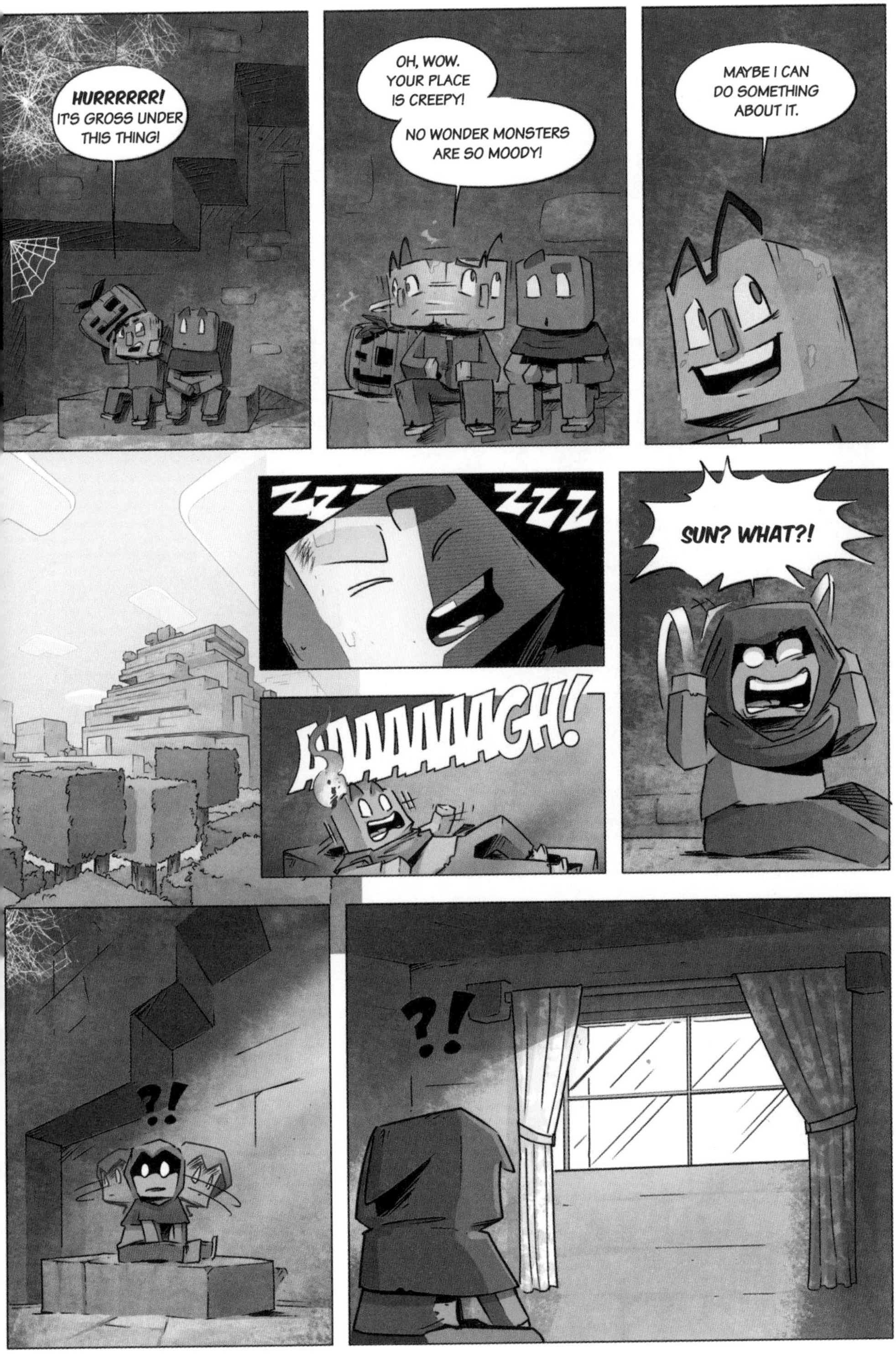
HURRRRRR! IT'S GROSS UNDER THIS THING!
OH, WOW. YOUR PLACE IS CREEPY!
NO WONDER MONSTERS ARE SO MOODY!
MAYBE I CAN DO SOMETHING ABOUT IT.
ZZZ ZZZ
AAAAAAAAGH!
SUN? WHAT?!
?!
?!

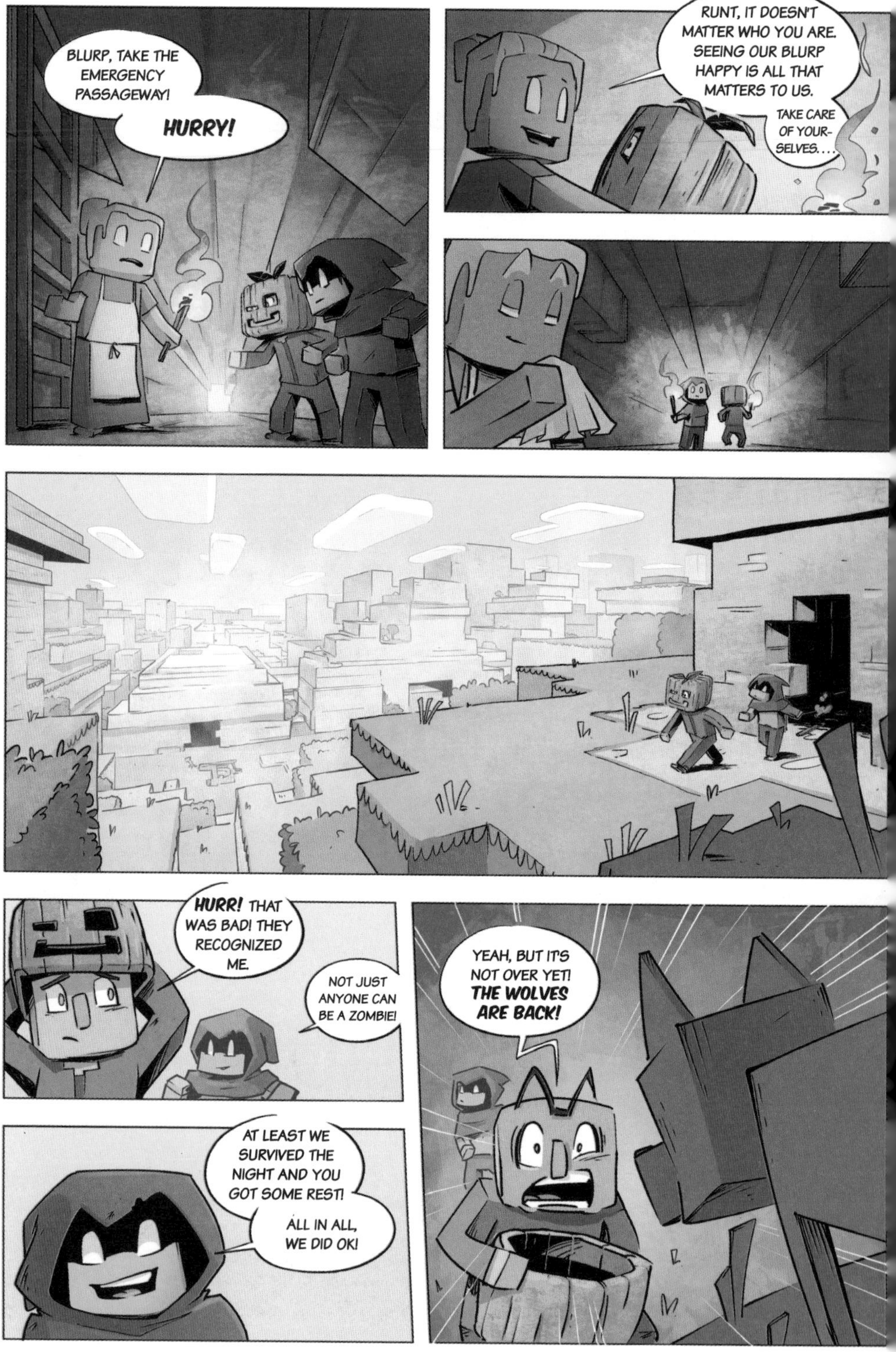
BLURP, TAKE THE EMERGENCY PASSAGEWAY!
HURRY!
RUNT, IT DOESN'T MATTER WHO YOU ARE. SEEING OUR BLURP HAPPY IS ALL THAT MATTERS TO US.
TAKE CARE OF YOURSELVES. . . .
HURR! THAT WAS BAD! THEY RECOGNIZED ME.
NOT JUST ANYONE CAN BE A ZOMBIE!
AT LEAST WE SURVIVED THE NIGHT AND YOU GOT SOME REST!
ALL IN ALL, WE DID OK!
YEAH, BUT IT'S NOT OVER YET! THE WOLVES ARE BACK!

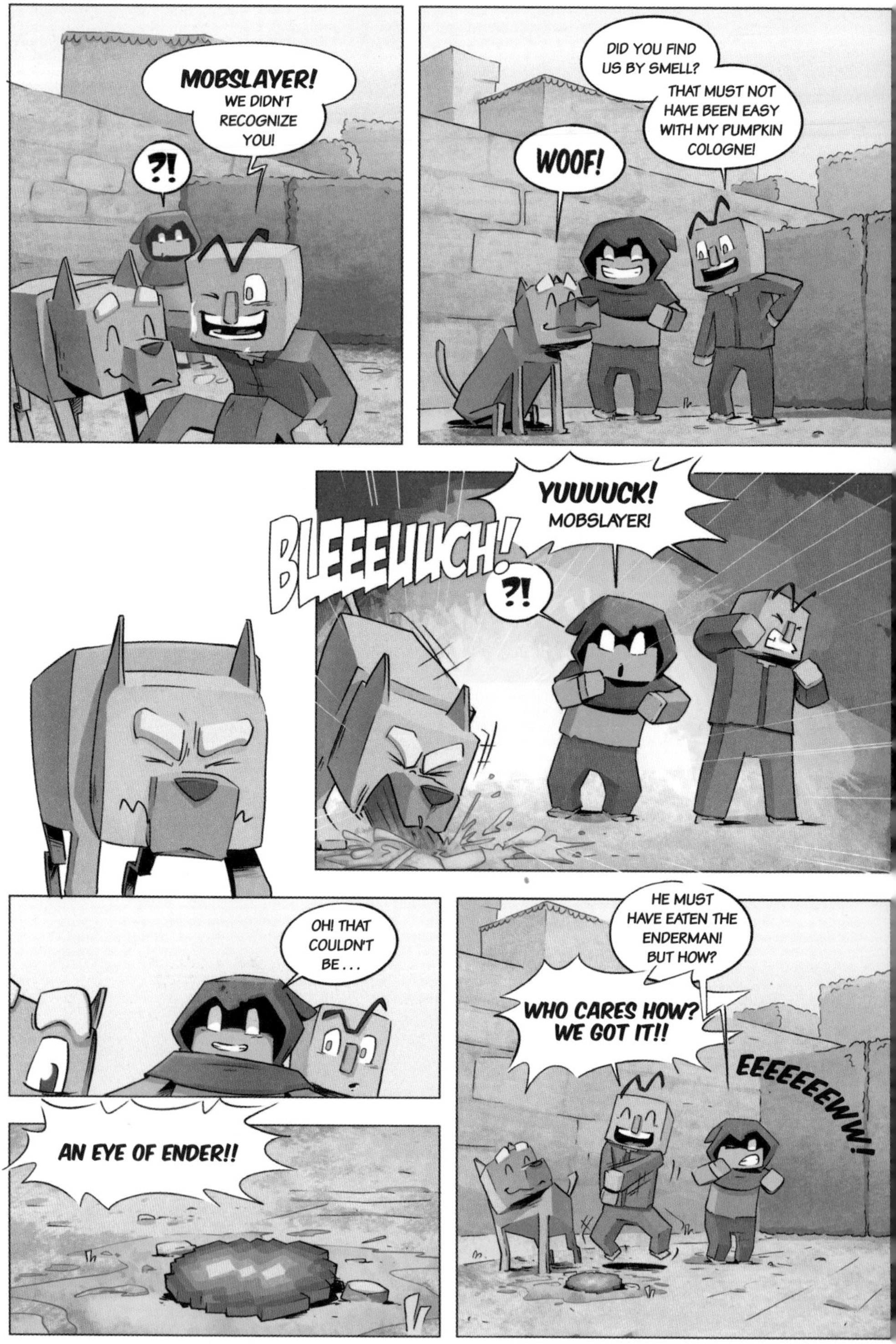
MOBSLAYER! WE DIDN'T RECOGNIZE YOU!
?!
DID YOU FIND US BY SMELL?
THAT MUST NOT HAVE BEEN EASY WITH MY PUMPKIN COLOGNE!
WOOF!
BLEEEUUCH!
YUUUUCK! MOBSLAYER!
?!
OH! THAT COULDN'T BE . . .
AN EYE OF ENDER!!
HE MUST HAVE EATEN THE ENDERMAN! BUT HOW?
WHO CARES HOW? WE GOT IT!!
EEEEEEEEWW!

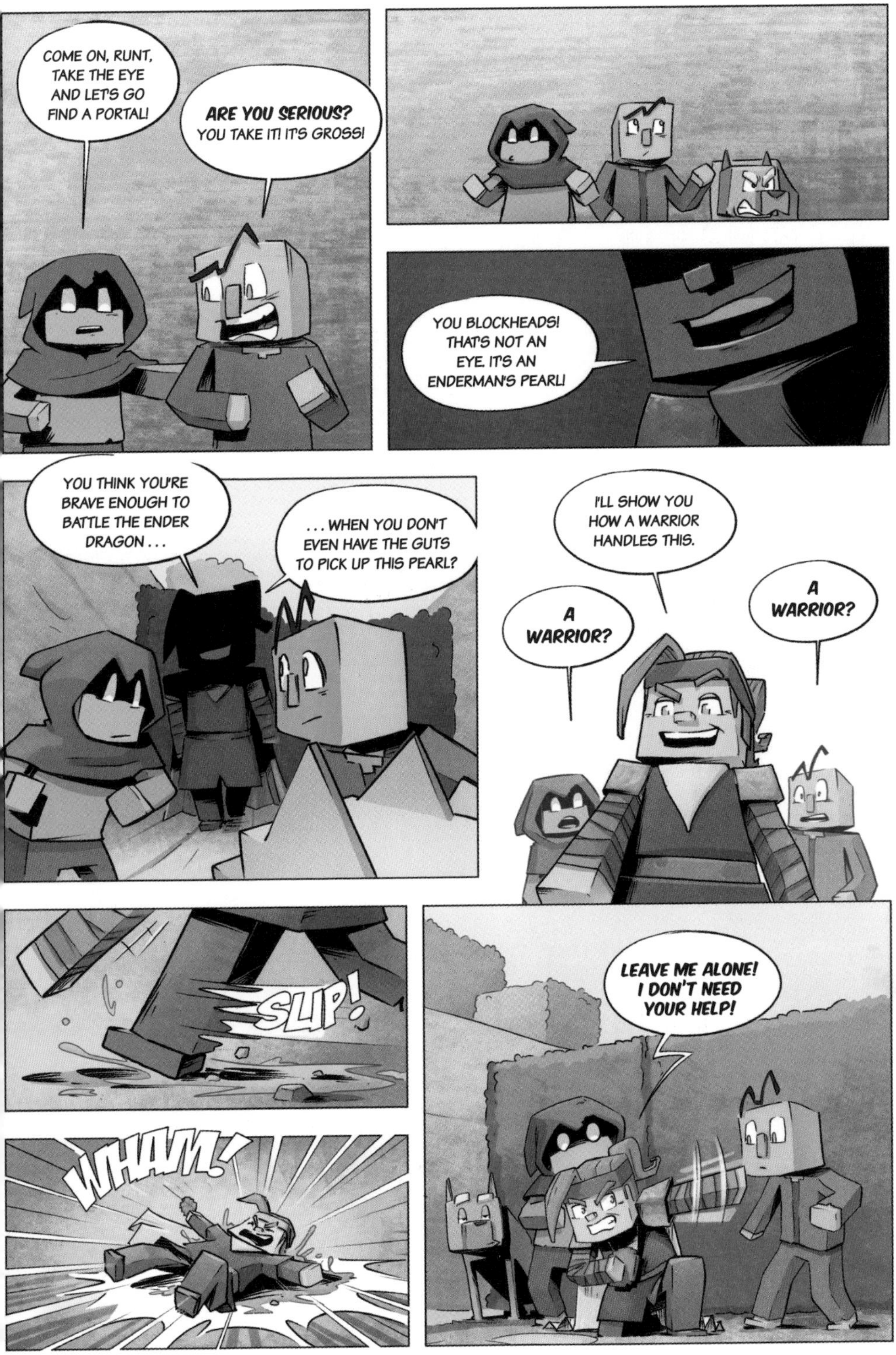
COME ON, RUNT, TAKE THE EYE AND LET'S GO FIND A PORTAL!
ARE YOU SERIOUS? YOU TAKE IT! IT'S GROSS!
YOU BLOCKHEADS! THAT'S NOT AN EYE. IT'S AN ENDERMAN'S PEARL!
YOU THINK YOU'RE BRAVE ENOUGH TO BATTLE THE ENDER DRAGON . . .
. . . WHEN YOU DON'T EVEN HAVE THE GUTS TO PICK UP THIS PEARL?
I'LL SHOW YOU HOW A WARRIOR HANDLES THIS.
A WARRIOR?
A WARRIOR?
SLIP!
WHAM!
LEAVE ME ALONE! I DON'T NEED YOUR HELP!

LOOK AT THIS PICTURE. DO YOU KNOW WHAT THIS THING SURROUNDED BY RODS IS?

IS IT AN UPSIDE-DOWN MONSTER?

NO! IT'S A BLAZE! YOU GET AN EYE OF ENDER BY MERGING THE PEARL WITH POWDER FROM THIS MONSTER'S RODS!

AND DO YOU KNOW WHERE YOU CAN FIND A BLAZE?

IN YOUR OLD BOOKS?

I'VE HEARD OF THAT—IT'S REALLY DANGEROUS!

IN THE NETHER! YOU MUST VENTURE INTO THAT INFERNAL DIMENSION!

I THINK WE NEED A PORTAL. THOSE ARE HARD TO MAKE AND HARDER TO FIND. . . .

OH, YOU MEAN ONE OF THESE?

OH NO! MY CURTAIN!

RIIIPP!

THAT'S ENOUGH! GIVE IT BACK!

CRASH!

BONK!

WHAM!

THUD!

THE LACK OF RESPECT...

OK, FINE. YOU'RE RIGHT.

WHEN I WAS YOUNGER, I DREAMED OF BECOMING A WARRIOR.

I MEMORIZED ALL THE BOOKS, ALL THE BATTLE TACTICS.

I KNEW EVERYTHING THERE WAS TO KNOW ABOUT MONSTERS!

BUT WHENEVER IT CAME TIME TO PUT IT INTO PRACTICE, IT GOT COMPLICATED....

EVERY DAY THERE WAS SOME NEW DISASTER OR TERRIBLE MISTAKE.

GOING THROUGH THE PORTAL

HAS ALWAYS BEEN A DREAM OF MINE ... BUT IT'S BETTER FOR EVERYONE IF I JUST STAY HERE.

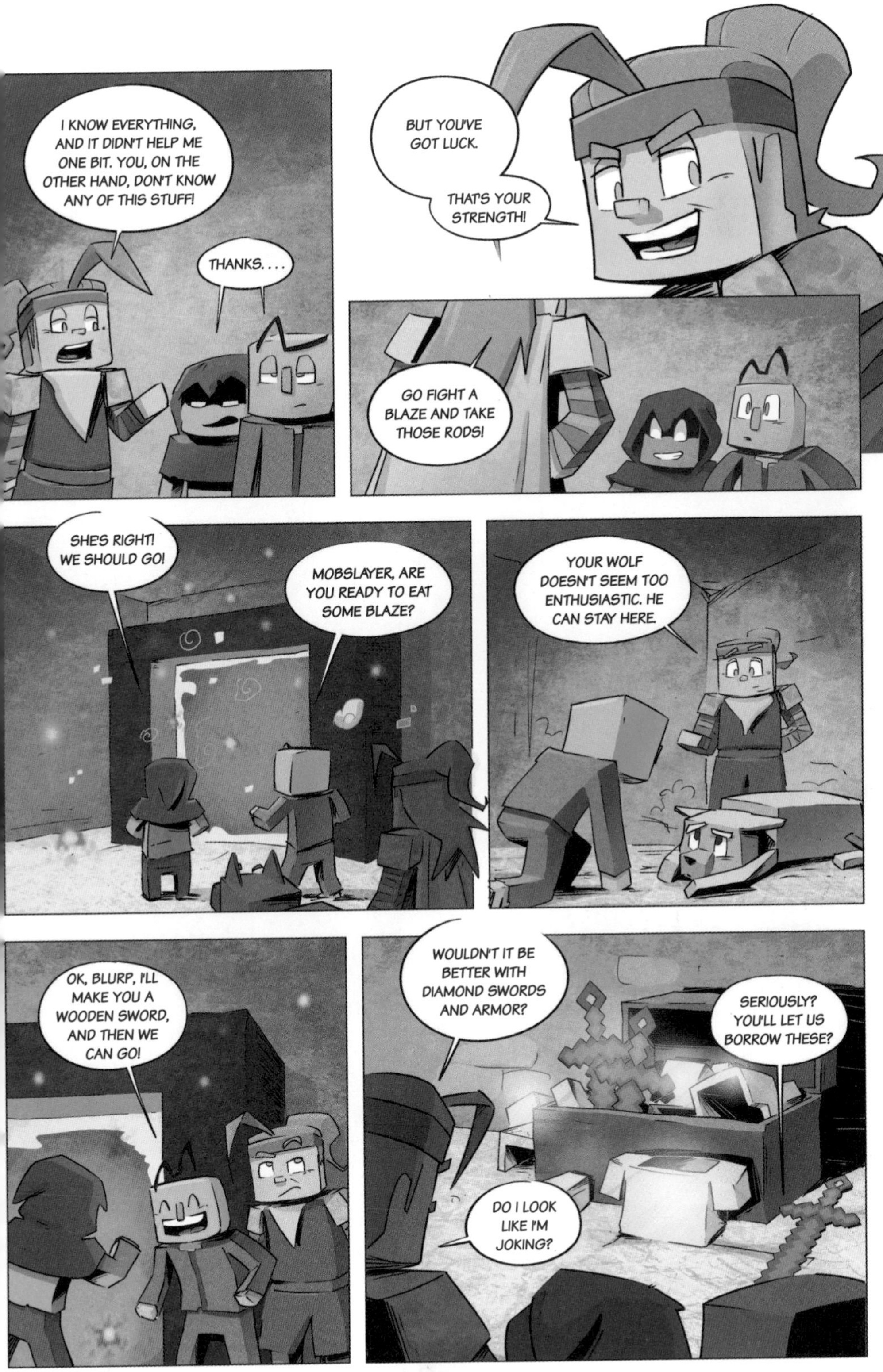
I KNOW EVERYTHING, AND IT DIDN'T HELP ME ONE BIT. YOU, ON THE OTHER HAND, DON'T KNOW ANY OF THIS STUFF!
THANKS. . . .
BUT YOU'VE GOT LUCK.
THAT'S YOUR STRENGTH!
GO FIGHT A BLAZE AND TAKE THOSE RODS!
SHE'S RIGHT! WE SHOULD GO!
MOBSLAYER, ARE YOU READY TO EAT SOME BLAZE?
YOUR WOLF DOESN'T SEEM TOO ENTHUSIASTIC. HE CAN STAY HERE.
OK, BLURP, I'LL MAKE YOU A WOODEN SWORD, AND THEN WE CAN GO!
WOULDN'T IT BE BETTER WITH DIAMOND SWORDS AND ARMOR?
SERIOUSLY? YOU'LL LET US BORROW THESE?
DO I LOOK LIKE I'M JOKING?

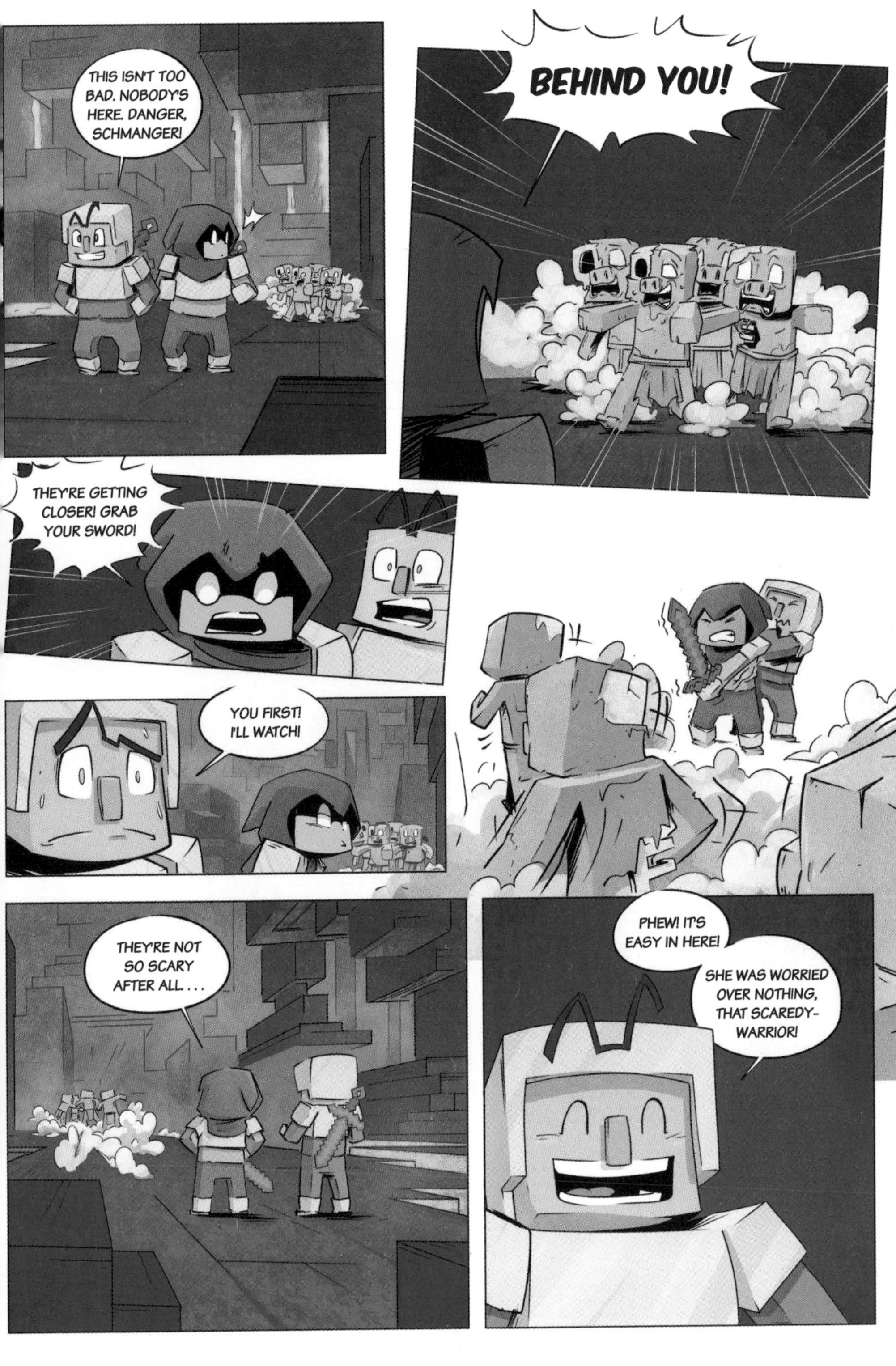
THIS ISN'T TOO BAD. NOBODY'S HERE. DANGER, SCHMANGER!
BEHIND YOU!
THEY'RE GETTING CLOSER! GRAB YOUR SWORD!
YOU FIRST! I'LL WATCH!
THEY'RE NOT SO SCARY AFTER ALL . . .
PHEW! IT'S EASY IN HERE!
SHE WAS WORRIED OVER NOTHING, THAT SCAREDY-WARRIOR!

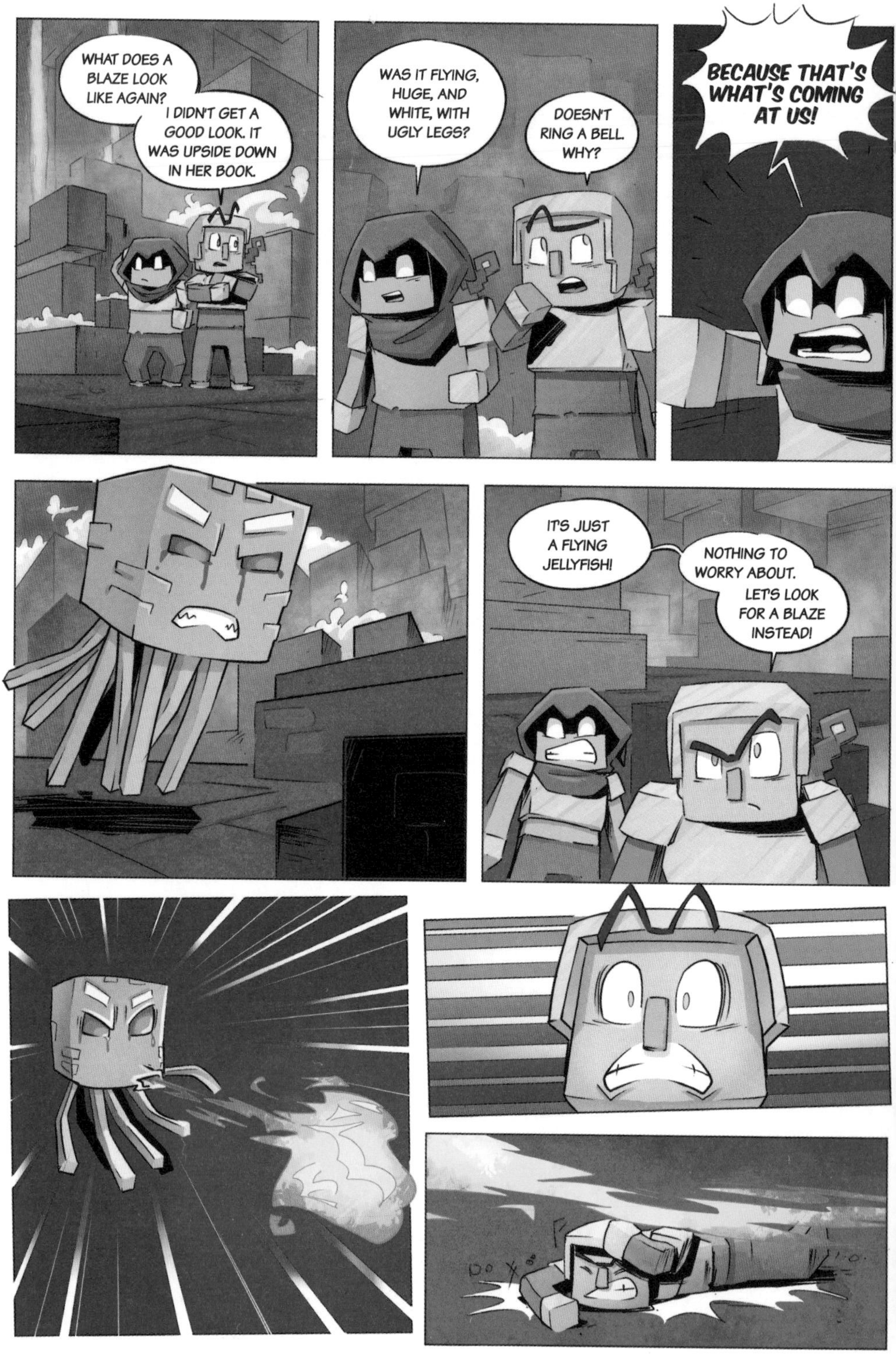
WHAT DOES A BLAZE LOOK LIKE AGAIN?
I DIDN'T GET A GOOD LOOK. IT WAS UPSIDE DOWN IN HER BOOK.
WAS IT FLYING, HUGE, AND WHITE, WITH UGLY LEGS?
DOESN'T RING A BELL. WHY?
BECAUSE THAT'S WHAT'S COMING AT US!
IT'S JUST A FLYING JELLYFISH!
NOTHING TO WORRY ABOUT.
LET'S LOOK FOR A BLAZE INSTEAD!

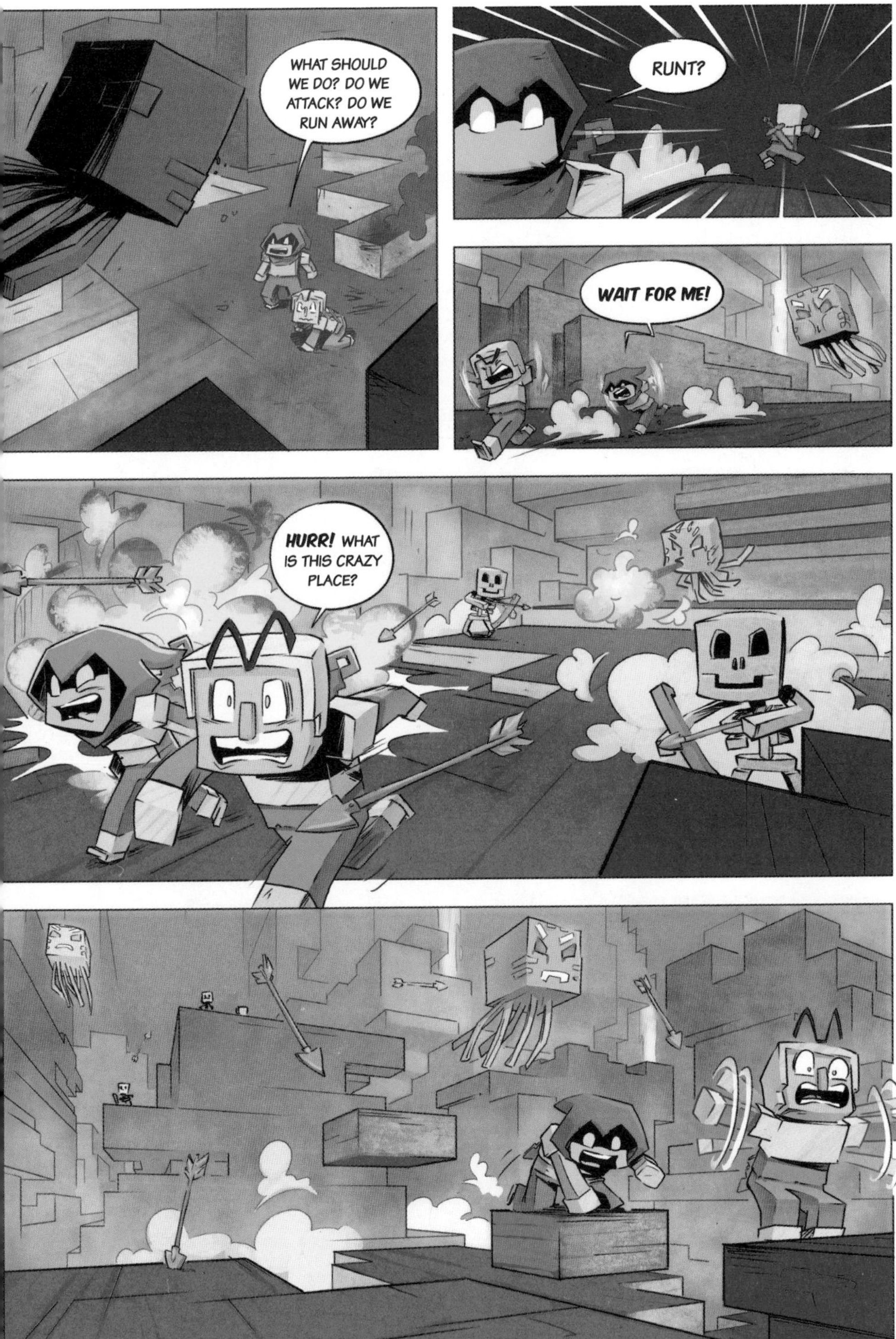
WHAT SHOULD WE DO? DO WE ATTACK? DO WE RUN AWAY?
RUNT?
WAIT FOR ME!
HURR! WHAT IS THIS CRAZY PLACE?

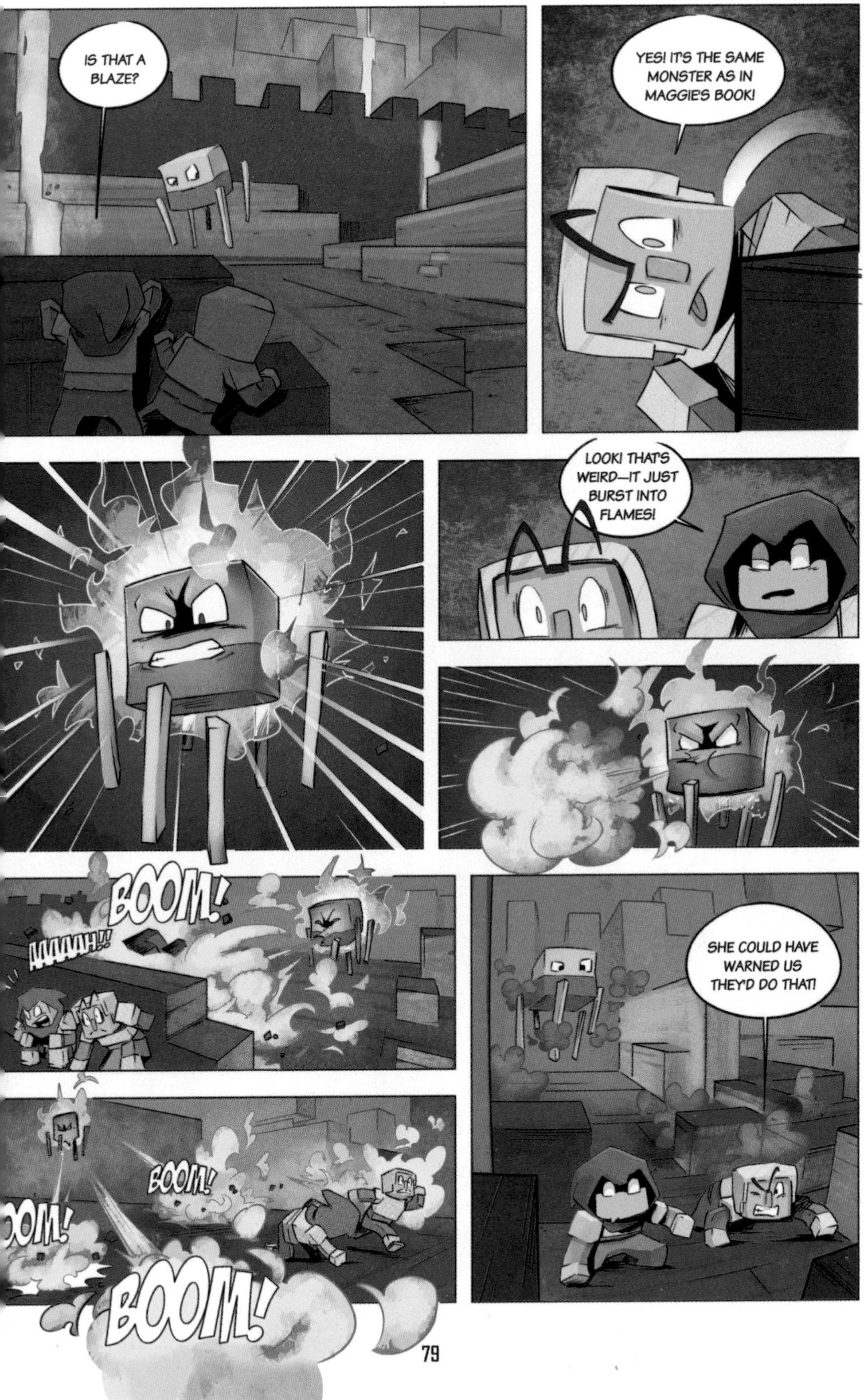
IS THAT A BLAZE?
YES! IT'S THE SAME MONSTER AS IN MAGGIE'S BOOK!
LOOK! THAT'S WEIRD—IT JUST BURST INTO FLAMES!
BOOM!
AAAAAH!!
BOOM!
OOM!
BOOM!
SHE COULD HAVE WARNED US THEY'D DO THAT!

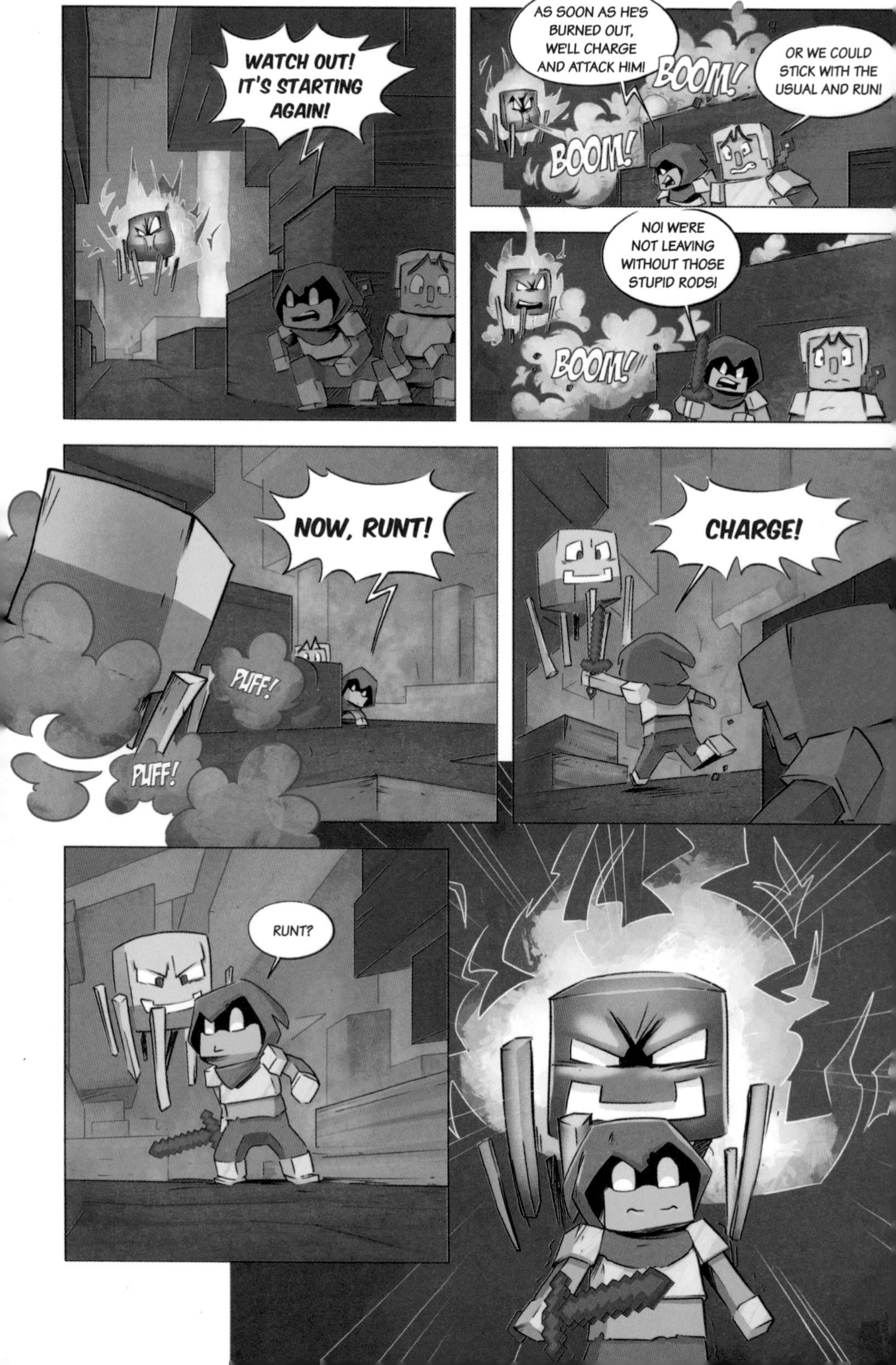
WATCH OUT! IT'S STARTING AGAIN!
AS SOON AS HE'S BURNED OUT, WE'LL CHARGE AND ATTACK HIM!
BOOM!
OR WE COULD STICK WITH THE USUAL AND RUN!
BOOM!
NO! WE'RE NOT LEAVING WITHOUT THOSE STUPID RODS!
BOOM!
NOW, RUNT!
PUFF!
PUFF!
CHARGE!
RUNT?

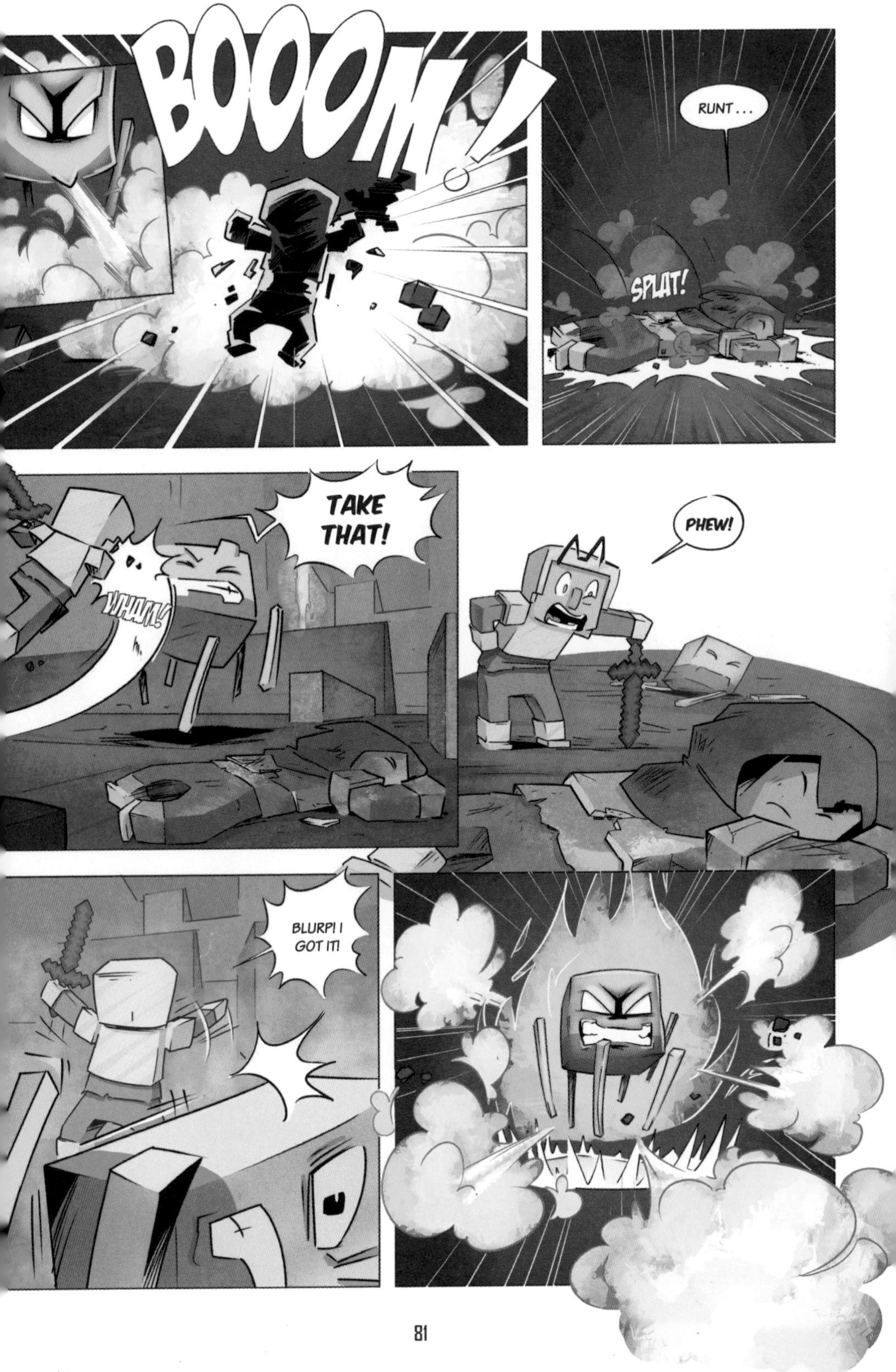
BOOOM!
RUNT . . .
SPLAT!
TAKE THAT!
WHAM!
PHEW!
BLURP! I GOT IT!

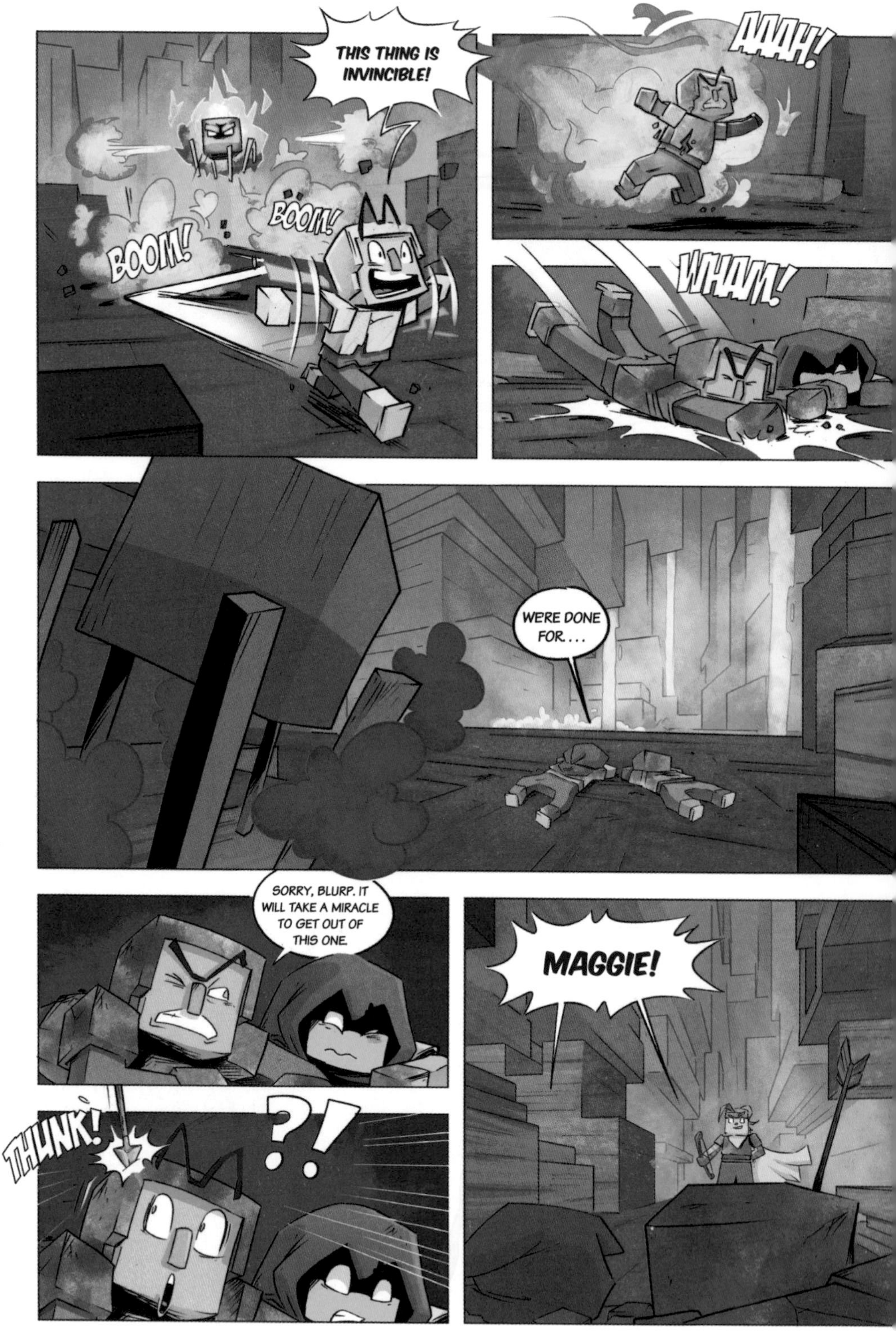
THIS THING IS INVINCIBLE!
BOOM!
BOOM!
AAAH!
WHAM!
WE'RE DONE FOR. . . .
SORRY, BLURP. IT WILL TAKE A MIRACLE TO GET OUT OF THIS ONE.
THUNK!
?!
MAGGIE!

I THINK WE'RE STILL WAITING ON THAT MIRACLE.

HA! HA! HA!
HA!
HA!
HA!

TINK!

THUNK

POOF!

CLINK!

CLINK!

CLINK!

CLINK!

MAGGIE! YOU DID IT! YOU GOT THE BLAZE!!

SEE! YOU MADE IT TO THE NETHER AFTER ALL!

IF NOOBS LIKE YOU CAN DO IT, SO CAN I!

YOU'RE HURT!

YOU'RE AMAZING!

YEAH, I HAD TO DEAL WITH A FEW MONSTERS ON THE WAY HERE. . . .

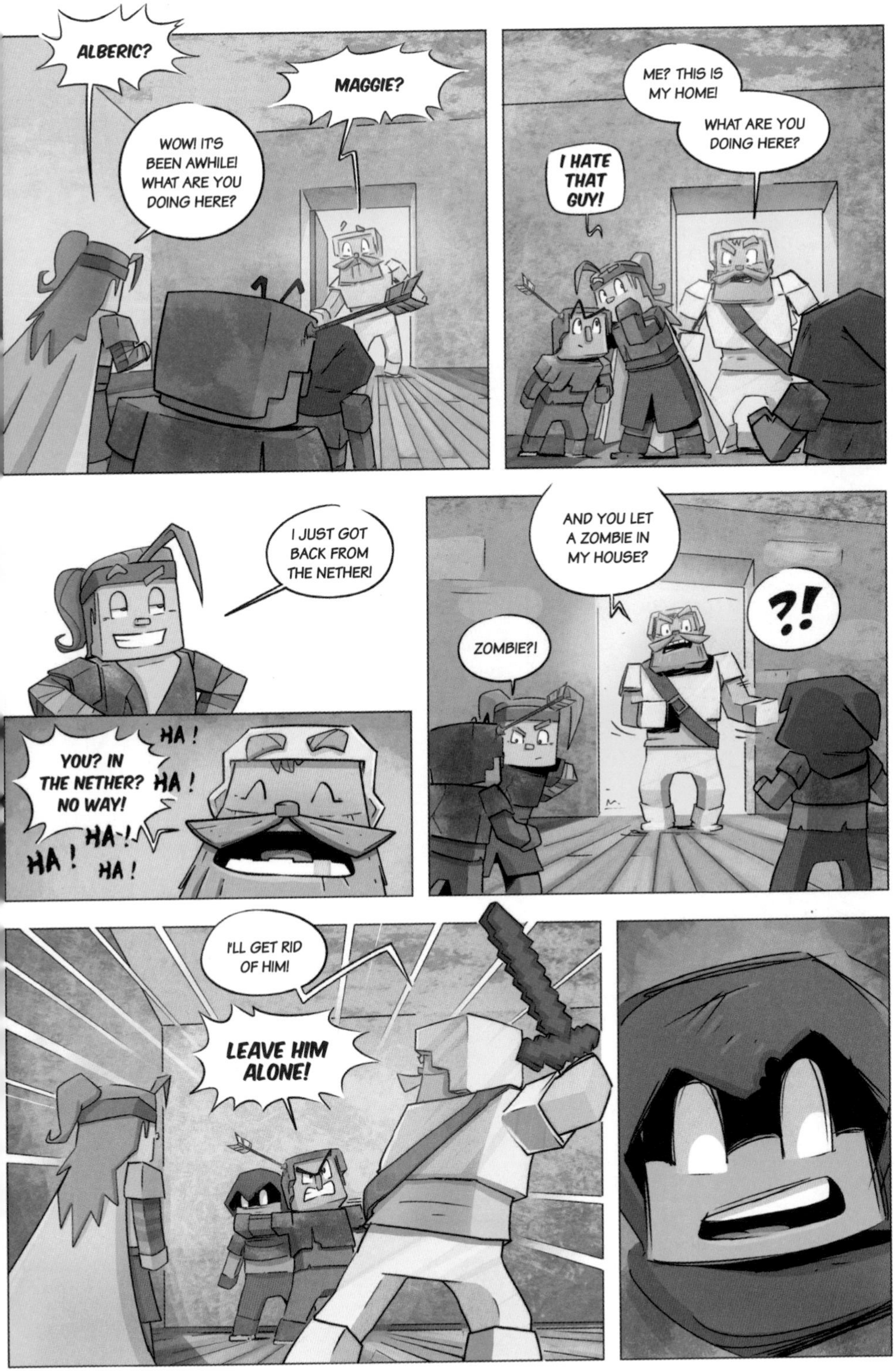
ALBERIC?
MAGGIE?
WOW! IT'S BEEN AWHILE! WHAT ARE YOU DOING HERE?
ME? THIS IS MY HOME!
WHAT ARE YOU DOING HERE?
I HATE THAT GUY!
I JUST GOT BACK FROM THE NETHER!
YOU? IN THE NETHER? NO WAY!
HA! HA! HA-! HA! HA!
AND YOU LET A ZOMBIE IN MY HOUSE?
ZOMBIE?!
?!
I'LL GET RID OF HIM!
LEAVE HIM ALONE!

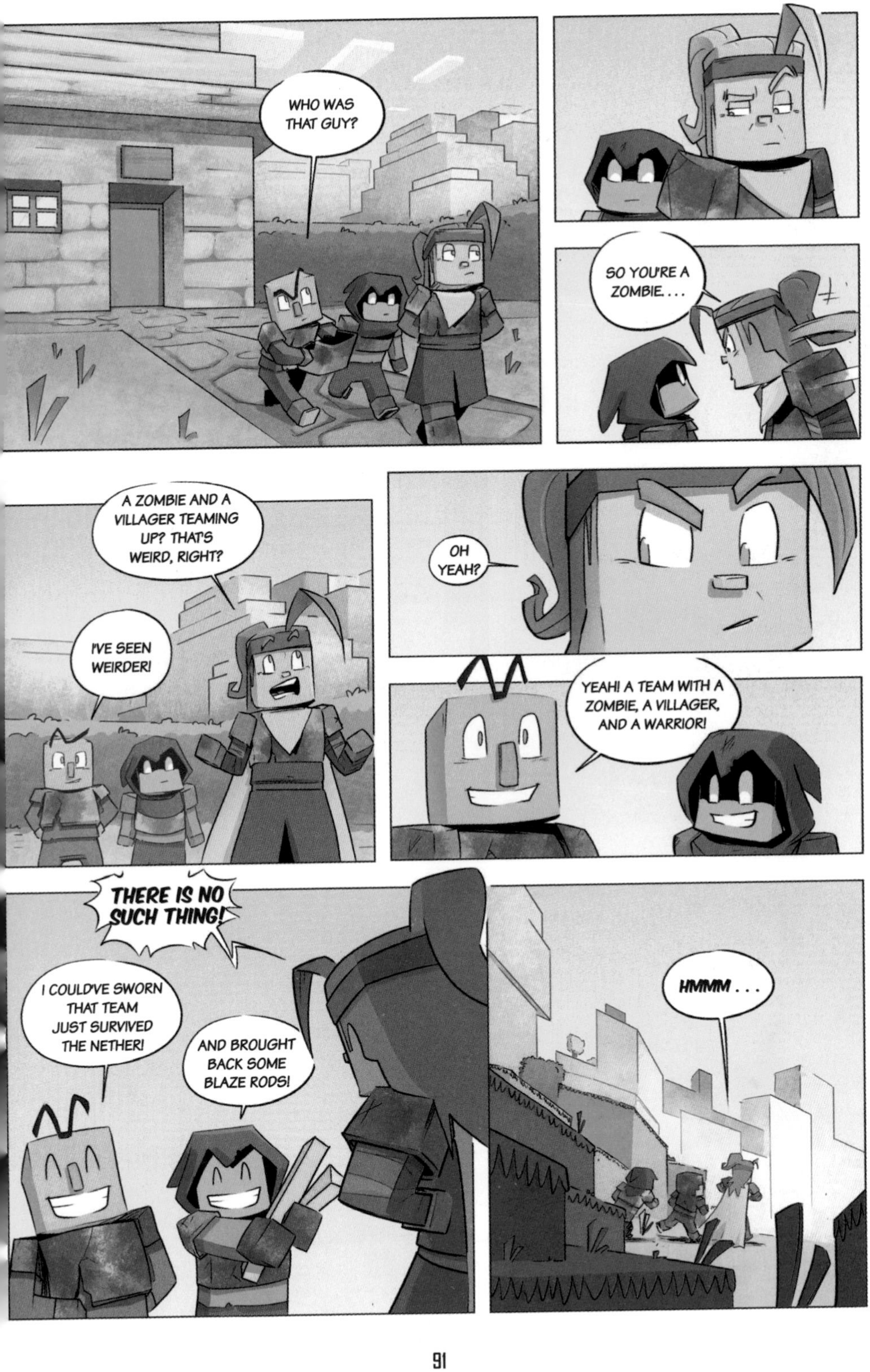

WHO WAS THAT GUY?
SO YOU'RE A ZOMBIE. . . .
A ZOMBIE AND A VILLAGER TEAMING UP? THAT'S WEIRD, RIGHT?
I'VE SEEN WEIRDER!
OH YEAH?
YEAH! A TEAM WITH A ZOMBIE, A VILLAGER, AND A WARRIOR!
THERE IS NO SUCH THING!
I COULD'VE SWORN THAT TEAM JUST SURVIVED THE NETHER!
AND BROUGHT BACK SOME BLAZE RODS!
HMMM . . .

ABOUT THE AUTHORS

PIRATE SOURCIL is a comic book author known for his blog and his comic series *Le Joueur du grenier*, published by Hugo BD. He is also a fan of geek literature and passionate about the world of gaming.

After studying carpentry, **JEZ** turned to drawing and graphic design and decided to make a career out of it.

ODONE is a French illustrator and specializes in adding color to many comic books.

DIARY OF AN 8-BIT WARRIOR

DIARY OF AN 8-BIT VILLAGER

Runt, the villager who wants to be a warrior (like Steve)

CUBE KID

AN UNOFFICIAL MINECRAFT ADVENTURE

DIARY OF AN 8-BIT WARRIOR: FROM SEEDS TO SWORDS

The continuing adventures of Runt, the villager turned warrior

CUBE KID

AN UNOFFICIAL MINECRAFT ADVENTURE

DIARY OF AN 8-BIT WARRIOR: CRAFTING ALLIANCES

Adventure continues for Runt, the village warrior

CUBE KID

AN UNOFFICIAL MINECRAFT ADVENTURE

DIARY OF AN 8-BIT WARRIOR: PATH OF THE DIAMOND

Runt's journey is coming to an end!

CUBE KID

AN UNOFFICIAL MINECRAFT ADVENTURE

DIARY OF AN 8-BIT WARRIOR: QUEST MODE

CUBE KID

AN UNOFFICIAL MINECRAFT ADVENTURE

DIARY OF AN 8-BIT WARRIOR: FORGING DESTINY

CUBE KID

AN UNOFFICIAL MINECRAFT ADVENTURE

AND MEET EEEBS, THE MOST NOOBIEST CAT IN OVERWORLD!

TALES OF AN 8-BIT KITTEN: LOST IN THE NETHER

Follow the adventures of Eeebs, the noobiest cat in all of Minecraft

CUBE KID

AN UNOFFICIAL MINECRAFT ADVENTURE

TALES OF AN 8-BIT KITTEN: A CALL TO ARMS

See what happens next to Eeebs, the most disobedient cat in all of Minecraft

CUBE KID

AN UNOFFICIAL MINECRAFT ADVENTURE